D0978522

Endless Love
The Love Series
Part Three

Emma Keene

THIS BOOK IS THE PROPERTY OF
THE NATIONAL CITY PUBLIC LIBRARY
1401 NATIONAL CITY BLVD
NATIONAL CITY, CA 91950

Copyright © 2014 Outfox Digital Publishing

All rights reserved.

ISBN: 1499685254
ISBN-13: 978-1499685251

DEDICATION

This book is dedicated to my husband and our two dogs. They keep me sane while I write. Their distractions are always welcome. I love you three, you're the best family I could have ever asked for.

CONTENTS

CHAPTER ONE

I open my eyes and look around. It takes me a minute to realize where I am. I guess I must have fallen asleep on the floor after a while of crying while curled up in a ball.

Ugh. I look at the clock, it's five in the morning and I have a feeling there's no point in going back to sleep.

I sit up and look around for my phone. I see it on the floor, smashed into pieces. I pick up the biggest three, which includes most of the screen, and toss them into the trash. Dex is going to be upset that I broke the new phone he gave me.

The only thing that makes me feel better about the phone is that I can't reread the texts that Logan sent me. I still can't believe it... it feels like a bad dream that I'm never going to wake up from.

I do the only thing I can think of. I put on my bathing suit, wrap a towel around myself and head downstairs. I know the water is going to be brutally cold and I don't care.

When my toes touch the water, I want to cry out. It's colder than the water in a swimming pool should ever be. I put my arms on the side of the pool and take a deep breath. I push my feet against the wall and dive under the water as I force myself to start swimming. With any luck, it'll help me clear my head and I'll actually be able to focus today. As much as I would love to just stay in bed all day, I know that we have a movie to shoot and Dex is counting on me.

I finish three laps before I can't take it anymore. I feel like I've lost the will to move my arms and legs.

I get out of the pool, dry myself off and sit down in one of the chairs and bury my face in my hands as I start to cry. I can't help it. It still feels surreal that Logan just broke up with me. I can't believe I'm never going to see him again. I get that it's partly my fault… I did go out for coffee with Spencer, but I wish that Logan would at least let me explain myself.

"What's wrong?"

I turn to Dex, who is standing just a few feet away from me. He has a towel wrapped around his waist and he looks like he's ready to go for a swim. When Dex sees the look on my face, he sits down on the chair next to me and puts his hand on my shoulder. Normally I would be embarrassed about him seeing me in my swimsuit, but I'm so out of sorts that I don't even care.

The look on his face says everything. I can tell that he's actually concerned about me… maybe more so than my mom has ever been. It's a weird feeling, but I'm glad.

"What is it?" he says, asking again.

I shake my head. I already know how much pressure he's under with his movie and there's no way I can tell him about my problems. Not to mention he's been so nice and taken a huge risk by casting me.

"Just tell me… you're the star of my film and I've gotta make sure my star is happy."

I look into his eyes and he smiles at me. I use the back of my hand to wipe the last tears as they fall on my cheek and I take a deep breath.

"My boyfriend… he… broke up with me."

Hearing the words trickle out of my mouth makes me

want to cry again, but I force myself to breathe and stay calm.

"I'm sorry to hear that... his name was Logan, right?"

I nod. I'm kind of surprised actually that Dex remembers considering how much he's got on his plate.

"Well... do you think it would help if you took a couple of days off from the movie and go back to Salem?"

I wrinkle my forehead. I'm not sure what he means... I know that we are already way behind on the film and there's no way we can afford to stop for me to go back to Salem. Not to mention, I'm not getting paid until we finish the movie and I don't have the money to get back there.

"No...."

"Is it about the money?"

"What do you mean?"

"Would you go back if you had the money?" he says.

I look into his eyes and I can tell that he's not going to be upset or judge me if I tell him the truth. I can't do it though, I have to lie to him.

"No... I don't want to ever go back there."

I feel my heart breaking. I know that if I could just see Logan I would be able to explain it all to him and make him understand, he would have to understand, and then he would take me back.

Dex looks at me for a long moment and then just nods. I have a feeling that he can see right through me and I really do want to tell him the truth... I just can't do it. I can't leave now, not after everything that he's done for me.

"If you change your mind, let me know and I'll charter the plane for you."

"Thanks, but I don't need to ever talk to him again."

Dex nods and stands up. He walks toward the edge of the pool, stops and turns around. He looks at me and I can tell he knows that I want to go back to Salem. He opens his mouth to say something, but closes it again. Dex lets the towel wrapped around his waist fall to the ground and he dives into the pool.

Once he starts to swim, I start to cry again. I hate myself for what I just did. Dex didn't deserve that. Not after he's been so amazingly kind to me.

I stand up and head back inside so that I don't have to talk to Dex. I need to be alone for a few minutes while I think about it all. I wish I would have told him, I really do, but now I can't. I just have to try to push Logan out of my mind and focus on the movie… nothing else makes sense right now.

I close my bedroom door and sit down on my bed. I take out my backup phone and turn it on. The keys feel cheap and it makes me miss my new phone already. I know that I have to tell Dex I broke it, it's the only way he has to get a hold of me.

Tears start to form in my eyes, but I push them away and try to calm myself down. *Get a hold of yourself, Amy.*

I really just feel like I can't take it anymore—it seems like every single time things start to look up, something awful happens that brings my world crashing down. I hope that things will start to get better.

After my shower, I throw on some jeans and a T-shirt. I head downstairs to the kitchen. Dex is already down here and dressed.

"Hey," he says, "you feel any better?"

He smiles at me as he takes another sip of his coffee before setting his mug down.

I shrug. I feel awful, but I can't bring myself to say anything to him. I need to focus on making it through the day.

"o you want to take today off"?

"No."

"Are you sure?"

I nod and look away from Dex. I know if he looks into my eyes, he will be able to tell exactly what's going on with me and what I'm thinking about.

"I guess let's get going. We have some big scenes to shoot today."

I follow Dex out of the kitchen, to the garage and we get into his car. I let my thoughts wander as he pulls out of the garage and starts driving to the set. Today is going to be rough... I have no idea how I'm going to even deliver my lines and do a good job. I don't have a choice, though, I can't let Dex down.

"I didn't tell your mom, by the way."

I turn to Dex, a little surprised by what he's just said, but he's focused on driving.

"No?"

"No... I was talking to her and it just didn't seem like the right moment. She was going on and on about how one of her friends had talked about her behind her back to another friend. She was already in such a bad mood that I didn't want to bring it up."

I get it, but I'm worried that she's going to find out and then she's really going to be upset. Hopefully Dex will tell her tonight when we get home. I feel like the longer we don't tell her the worse it's going to be.

"That makes sense," I say.

I can see Dex nodding out of the corner of my eye and I have a feeling he's thinking the same thing I am.

Dex pulls the car into his spot at the lot and we get out of the car. He looks at me and opens his mouth, but closes it again and turns away as she shoves his keys into his pocket. I head toward my trailer, I don't have the time to stop and think about what he could have possibly been about to say.

My clothes for the day, jeans and T-shirt and my black flats, are already sitting in my trailer and I get changed quickly. I leave and head over to hair and makeup, since I'm already running a few minutes late. Leslie is waiting for me when I walk in.

"Hey, Hun, how are you?" she says.

I force myself to smile and sit down in her chair.

"I'm fine."

I'm a little worried. It seems like the longer I'm in L.A.,

the easier it becomes to lie to people. That's not the person I want to be, but I feel like right now there's really no alternative.

Leslie sprays my hair with a bottle of water and then blows it dry. She styles my hair to look like it did last time and she takes a step back to make sure it looks right.

"Are you sure?" she says.

I should tell her the truth… there's no reason why I shouldn't. I open my mouth, but a knock on the door interrupts me before I say anything.

"Come in!" Leslie says.

The door swings open and a guy comes in. He's young, maybe nineteen or twenty, and walks over to me.

"Amy?"

"Yes?"

He extends a script to me and turns to leave once I take it from him. I look down at the script and realize that it's for today… and it's pretty thick. I sigh and start to flip through the first few pages. I wish I could have had this earlier, it would have given me something to do when I couldn't sleep.

"Hun, do you mind setting that down for just a second? I can get your makeup done in like two minutes and then you're free."

I nod as I read one last line of the script and toss it on the table next to me. Today is going to be rough.

"Were you about to say something before that guy came with your script?"

"Yeah," I say, realizing that Leslie is a good person to talk to about this. "My boyfriend… he broke up with me last night."

"Oh, Hun, that's awful! How could Spencer do that to you?"

I shake my head and hold back a laugh.

"No, not Spencer."

I look up at Leslie and she has a confused look on her face. I forgot that she saw the entertainment program and

6

even though I told her I wasn't dating him, she apparently didn't believe me.

"I thought...."

"No, I was dating this guy back in Salem. I met him and then I had to come here... it's a long story, but basically he broke up with me because he saw that story about Spencer and me. He didn't believe me when I told him nothing was going on between us."

Leslie shakes her head, sits down on the chair next to me and puts her hand on my knee. Her touch makes me feel safe.

"Well, I'm not an expert on keeping men, but I can tell you this much... if he's not smart enough to trust you and believe you when you tell him something, then he's not worth your time."

She squeezes my knee and smiles at me. I force myself to smile back, even though right now I would much rather cry.

"I'm serious. There's so many guys out there... you can't worry about what one guy thinks or says."

I wish I could believe what she's saying, but Logan wasn't just some guy. He helped me through so much with Mitch and with my dad dying. No matter what the rest of my life holds, Logan will always hold a special place in my heart and I'll never forget him.

A tear starts to form in my eye and I quickly wipe it away with my finger and take a deep breath.

I've gotta get myself together. I don't have time for this today.

CHAPTER TWO

Today was impossibly long and I'm so glad it's over. I wasn't sure that I was even going to be able to make it through the whole thing... the moment I saw Spencer I wanted to cry. He was being impossibly nice and that made it even harder.

I splash the cool water on my face three times before reaching for the towel. It's strange to be standing in the bathroom of my very own trailer. It's nothing to write home about, it's pretty cramped and small, but it's mine and it's the only place where I can get a few moments of peace and quiet during the day.

I want to blame Spencer for Logan breaking up with me, it was him that wanted to take me to coffee and shopping, but I know that's not fair. Spencer was being nice and was trying to get me the role in the movie. I should be thanking him really... and maybe someday I'll be able to bring myself to have that conversation with him.

When I finish drying my hands and face, I walk back into what is effectively the bedroom of the trailer and I change back into my own clothes. My whole body thanks me for changing out of the snug outfit. I put my costume on the couch in the living area and grab my purse, opening it up to make sure I have everything.

"Wallet… phone…."

Someone knocks on the door and it pulls my attention away from collecting my things.

"Yes?"

The door opens and Dex comes in. He smiles at me as he sits on the couch and motions for me to join him. I nod and sit down in the chair across from him.

"How are you doing?" he says.

I move my eyes up from the floor until they meet his. I can see he's doing much better than me and he actually looks like he's in a good mood.

"I'm alright… how about you?"

He shrugs and smiles again. Dex takes his phone out of his pocket, looks at it for a brief moment and then puts it back.

"I'm good, can't complain, and you were wonderful today."

I can't believe he actually thinks that. I thought I did awful and I was actually surprised that Dex didn't stop shooting at one point where I almost started to cry.

"Thanks."

"No, I'm serious."

I look away, realizing that he caught the tone in my voice that implied I didn't believe him.

"You had this raw emotion today," he says, "which I'm sure came from… from what happened last night. It was amazing and exactly what the character needed for the scenes we shot today."

I do my best to smile. It's nice to hear him say that, but I'm not entirely convinced given how awful and out of sorts I felt today. Hopefully tomorrow will be better even though I feel like I have the weight of the world on my shoulders right now.

"I'm glad… It wasn't… never mind"

"What?"

I shake my head. I shouldn't have said anything. Part of

me wanted to tell Dex how hard of a time I'm having between Logan and my mom, but I can't… not now. The more I think about it, the more I want to cry and I also don't want to burden Dex with my problems.

Dex stands up from the couch, smiles at me and walks toward the door. He grasps the handle and turns around.

"Do you want to go get some dinner?"

I hesitate. The longer I stay away from the house means I don't have to talk to my mom as much, but if I go out to dinner with Dex it means that Spencer will probably tag along. Even though I know none of the blame rests on his shoulders, with the whole Logan thing, working with him all day was hard enough. There were times I wanted to break down and cry or just run away and never go back.

"It'll just be the two of us, if that makes any difference," he says.

It does, but there's no way I'm going to admit that to Dex. I guess it makes sense to go to dinner with him… it delays having to talk to my mom just that much more, which I think is totally worth it.

"Sure… I guess."

Dex smiles and opens the door. I complete one last sweep of the living room of the trailer, to make sure I've got all my stuff, and follow him outside. I don't catch up to Dex until he's at his car. We both get in and he starts it. The security guard at the gate flashes us a smile as we drive through. Dex turns the car in the opposite direction of home and pulls into a gap in the traffic.

"I was thinking we could try *Delikat*… it's this really great German restaurant."

"Sure… that's fine with me."

I've never been to a German restaurant, so it should be kind of interesting. I hope the food isn't crazy weird.

"What?"

"Huh?"

"They way you answered… you sounded a little apprehensive. We can go somewhere else if you want."

Busted. Apparently I'm not nearly as good at hiding my emotions, which is something that I've learned rather quickly since being in Los Angeles. It's something that I wish I would have known about myself before moving here, that's for sure.

"No… it's totally fine. I was just thinking that I've never eaten at a German restaurant."

Dex lets out a little chuckle and I think I notice him shaking his head a little.

"What?" I say, "why's that funny?"

"Sorry, I wasn't laughing at that. I was just thinking about how everything has changed for you. L.A. is so different from everything you've known your whole life and so far you're tackling it like a trooper."

I wouldn't think of it that way… not after how everyone has treated me. I've felt moments away from having a nervous breakdown since the moment I got on the plane in Greenville. It's a feeling I hope will fade, but I don't have confidence in that. The people in L.A. have been so hit or miss and the unkind ones… they make life difficult.

"Oh."

Dex pulls the car into a parking spot and looks over at me.

"Sorry, I didn't mean to sound… condescending."

I turn to him and smile. He really is a good guy… I'm still feeling bad that I treated him so poorly when I first got here and I didn't know the whole story. I still think it's sinking in that he wasn't the one to ruin my family and that it was really my mom. I don't think I'll ever be able to forgive her for that.

"No… it's not that. I was just thinking about what you said."

We get out of the car and Dex holds the door of the restaurant open for me. Dex stands at my side as we wait for the hostess. She smiles when she sees us, I can tell she recognizes him, but she doesn't say anything.

"Two?"

Dex nods as the woman picks up two menus from the stack behind her.

"Follow me, please."

She turns and heads into the dining room. The restaurant isn't packed, but it's busy and there are only a few empty tables that I can see. The hostess stops at a booth in the back corner and sets the menus down. We slide into the booth and I pick up the menu.

"Your server will be right with you."

"Thanks," Dex says.

I open the menu and quickly scan for anything that looks even remotely familiar. The names of all the dishes are in German, but the descriptions are all in English, thankfully, so I can kinda figure out what things are.

"Hi, I'm Alex and I'll be your server."

I look up from the menu. Alex has his order pad out as his eyes flick from me to Dex. I glance back down at the menu—I'm not even close to having any idea of what I want to eat.

"Are you ready to order? Or do you need a few more minutes?"

Dex closes his menu, sets it on the table in front of him and turns his attention to our server.

"Yes, I think we are."

I quickly look down at the menu and try to figure out what to order. I notice the silence from Alex and Dex and turn my attention back to them. They are both looking at me and I realize they are both waiting for me

"Umm…."

I look at Dex for some kind of guidance and he smiles at me and nods.

"We will both have the Gemischter Salat to start and the Nürnberger Bratwurst as our main."

As Alex writes down the order, I look through the menu until I find both of them. The first is a basic salad with cabbage, carrots, beets and potato salad. The bratwurst is just a grilled pork sausage with sauerkraut and mashed potatoes on the side. They both sound good and I'm starting to realize that I'm actually kind of hungry.

I smile at Dex and hand my menu to Alex.

"Anything to drink?"

"A bottle of water for the table... and I'll have a Pilsner, whatever you have on tap."

"Very good, Sir."

Alex scribbles on his pad before shoving it into his apron and flashing us a pearly smile. He walks away from the table and I turn my attention back to Dex.

"Thanks," I say.

"No problem. I come here a couple times a month, so I have a pretty good idea of what the best things to order are. I promise you're in good hands."

I have a feeling that I am... not only here, but also in terms of the movie and living in his house. I'm starting to feel like Dex cares about me more than my mom does. It's kind of weird to think that a man I barely know actually is looking out for me more than my only parent.

"Thanks."

He smiles back at me and reaches for the beer that Alex has just set down in front of him. Dex lifts the glass to his lips and takes a long drink.

"No problem."

"I'm so grateful that you've been so nice, to me. You let me come here and you've taken care of me and defended me...."

I stop and lower my head as I feel tears starting to well up in my eyes.

"Hey...."

I feel Dex's hand on mine. I can't bear to look up at him... I know that I'll start crying. I take a deep breath and calm myself down, I can't cry right now. Dex squeezes my hand and I finally look up at him when I'm sure that I won't start to bawl.

"It's all good. I'm glad that you're here. You've saved

me… and my film. I'll always owe you for that."

Even though Dex keeps telling me that I've saved the film, it's hard for me to believe I could have done something so positive and meaningful after all the shit that's happened in the last few months. I feel like when I look at him it's obvious that he's telling the truth and that makes me happier than I can ever express to him.

"Thanks."

"I'm serious… it's nice to know that there's still young people out there who care about something bigger than themselves."

I open my mouth to respond, but Alex sets down our salads on the table and refills my empty glass from the bottle. My stomach grumbles as I look at the food. Hopefully it wasn't loud enough for Dex to notice. I take a sip of water and pick up my fork.

"This looks good," I say, in an attempt to change the conversation. It's not that I'm not flattered by what he's saying, but I feel a little embarrassed about it. Not to mention it's hard to believe any adult could think I was so capable and worthy of such praise.

I take a bite of the salad, trying to get a mix of everything. A quiet moan escapes my lips and I look down, once again hoping that my apparent lack of table manners doesn't offend Dex.

"What do you think?"

I finish chewing the food in my mouth and smile at Dex.

"It's really good."

"I'm glad you think so. I don't eat here often enough and…."

I get the sense that Dex was about to say something else.

"What were you going to say?"

"Never mind."

I shrug and take another bite of salad. It really is very good. I'm starting to feel really spoiled… pretty much every single meal I've had since coming to L.A. has been delicious. It's definitely one of the things I'm going to miss when I do finally leave, but I'm not going to think about that right now.

Dex takes a few more bites of his salad before he sets his fork down. He drinks some of his beer and then clears his throat.

"What I was going to say was that I brought your mom here and she hated it... so I haven't been back since."

That's kind of sad. I must have a surprised look on my face because Dex chuckles and reaches for his beer again.

"Oh... well, that sucks."

"Yes, it does suck. Nothing I can do about it though... maybe you can come here again with me and that'll make up for it."

"I would like that."

I smile at Dex as I chew the last of my salad and push the bowl away. Alex stops to check on us and scoops up our empty bowls.

"How is everything so far?"

"Great," Dex says.

I smile at our server and nod.

"Another beer, Sir?"

Dex looks down at his nearly empty glass and squints as if the fate of the world rests on whether or not he's going to drink a second beer.

"I better not."

"Very good. Your main courses will be out in just a minute."

"Thanks," Dex says.

I'm glad that he's invited me to come here again with him. Going out to dinner with Dex has been nice. It feels calm... there's no pressure to order light, like when I went out to eat with my parents, and I don't have to worry about talking to a guy like when we go out with Spencer. Eating dinner out with Dex really is a nice experience.

"So... when do you think you'll tell my mom about me

being in your movie?"

Dex shrugs and picks his knife up off the table. He gently taps the base of it on the table. I have a feeling he's just fidgeting as he tries to think of the right thing to say.

"Sorry," I say, "we don't have to talk about it right now."

Alex is back and he sets down our main courses in front of us. There is a large bratwurst in the middle of the plate, with a large dollop of mustard on one end, and the sauerkraut and potatoes flank it on the plate.

"Can I get anything else for you?"

"Another bottle of water, please," Dex says.

"Right away, Sir."

I take the large steak knife off my plate and wrap my fingers around the polished handle. I feel bad for bringing up telling my mom... it's obvious that he's trying to avoid thinking about it. He did say he would be the one to tell her and I'm worried that the longer we wait the more upset she's going to be.

"No," Dex says, "we should talk about it. I can't put off telling your mom, it's not going to make it any better and I'm pretty sure it's just going to piss her off even more."

I crack a smile and so does Dex. He shakes his head and picks up his silverware. I don't get it... Dex is such a nice guy, what could he possibly see in my mom? I guess I'll never know because there's no way I'm going to ask him that.

"You're right... it's only going to get worse if you don't tell her."

Dex cuts a piece of his bratwurst, dips it in mustard and uses his knife to scoop some sauerkraut on top of it. I follow his lead and take my first bite of the bratwurst. The tanginess of the mustard and the sauerkraut complement it perfectly. I go for a spoonful of the potatoes as I finish chewing the bratwurst.

"What do you think?" Dex says.

I nod my head. It's really good, but my mouth is so full I can't answer without seeming like a heathen.

Dex smiles at me as he refills my water glass and then his own.

"I guess I better tell your mom tonight, when we get home."

"Yeah… I don't envy you."

Dex laughs as he cuts another piece of bratwurst.

"As you shouldn't. I'm going to do my best to explain the circumstances to her and she's going to have to understand. There's really no way around it because I want you in my movie and there's no way I'm budging on that."

He smiles at me and I smile back. For the first time since last night I'm actually happy about something—Dex is taking my side and coming to my defense against my mom. It's a great feeling that I won't forget anytime soon.

CHAPTER THREE

Dex puts his hand on the door handle and pauses. He takes a deep breath and I can tell he's not looking forward to telling my mom.

"Good luck," I say.

"Thanks. Are you going to bed?"

I open my mouth to answer, but instead I have to stifle a yawn. Today was a long day and it didn't help that I barely slept last night. I really hope that tonight I can push any thoughts of Logan out of my mind and get a good night's rest.

"I guess so."

Dex cracks a half hearted smile, but I can tell that he's already distracted by what he's going to tell my mom. I feel a little twinge of guilt, like I should be the one to tell her, but he said that he would.

"Alright... I'll see you down here tomorrow, at seven."

"Sounds good."

He flashes me another smile, this one seems a little more real, before he heads toward the kitchen. I slowly make my way up the stairs and let out a sigh of relief when I finally collapse onto my bed. My body is feeling the lack of sleep and the long day on set. I've gotta get a good night of sleep or I'm going to be in even worse shape tomorrow.

I take my cheap prepaid phone out of my purse and turn it on. I make a mental note to tell Dex that I broke the phone he gave me. There's a text from Jess waiting for me and I quickly pull it up.

Hey, I haven't heard from you lately and you didn't respond to my texts… so I figured I would give this number a try. Hopefully everything is good. Talk to you soon. Muah.

It's nice to get a text from her… it puts a smile on my face. I have no idea how long the text has been sitting there.

Sorry! I meant to text you back, but a lot has happened since we last talked. I broke my other phone, so it's back to this one.

I hesitate as I think about whether or not to say anything about Logan to Jess in the first message I sent her. I decide not to, in case she's busy or can't respond, and hit send. My phone chirps almost instantly with a reply from her.

Lol, how did you break your phone?

I take a deep breath and type out the message I've been dreading.

Logan… he broke up with me so I threw my phone on the floor and it basically exploded.

It hurts my heart to see the words. I hit send and look away from the phone. I'm still finding it hard to believe that my time with Logan was cut short first by my mom and now by him. I still wish he would have let me explain… I know I would have been able to change his mind. I look back at my phone as I get a reply from Jess.

Oh, I'm so sorry. Do you want to talk about it?

I feel like I've already talked about it more than I ever wanted to, but I have a feeling Jess will be able to offer some kind words, which I could definitely use now… especially since I'll have to face my mom at some point.

Logan saw a clip on YouTube of an entertainment show. It was a segment about Spencer and how he was spotted around town with his 'new girlfriend', which was me. He wouldn't answer my texts and when he finally did… that was when he broke up with me.

Wait… why were you hanging out with Spencer?

She has a point… I probably never should have gone out to coffee with him.

I got a job as Dex's assistant, so I saw Spencer on the movie set… when I got home at night my mom was there. Spencer texted to see if I would join him for coffee because he wanted to talk. I wanted to avoid my mom, so I agreed, and paparazzi spotted us when we were out. Logan accused me of cheating on him with Spencer.

Texting it to Jess brings all my emotions back to the surface. I really just want to curl up in bed and cry for a few weeks, but I don't have that luxury. I stare at my phone and wait for her to reply, but nothing comes. I wonder if she doesn't want to talk to me either.

I stand up and walk over to the window. I'll take any sort of distraction I can get at this point. The lights in the pool are already on and they shift to purple as I watch. It's still hard to believe this is where I live. I know it's not permanent, but I shouldn't take it for granted while I'm here. I have a feeling I'm going to miss this view once I'm back in Salem. My phone chirps and I look down.

I'm assuming, based on our last conversation about Spencer, that you were faithful to Logan. I just find it hard to believe that after everything you two went through, in such a short amount of time that he wouldn't even let you explain. I'm disappointed in him. If I see him on one of my runs, I'm going to talk to him about it.

I can't help but smile. Jess is so cute and protective of me. I wish that I had been able to spend more time with her when I was in Salem and I hope that we can hang out when I move back.

Don't worry about it. I'll just talk to him when I get back, if he wants anything to do with me. I'm still trying to process everything that happened and figure out what I'm doing next.

I take a deep breath and sit back down on my bed. I really hope that things will start to get easier, but I have a feeling that once I go back to Salem, and see Logan, they are going to be hard.

Are you sure? I really don't mind. I'll tell him to get his act together and listen to what you have to say.

I smile as I read her text. There's no doubt in my mind that she would do exactly that… which is not what I want. I do want to talk to Logan when I go back to Salem, I know that now, but I don't want him to talk to Jess because it might make things worse.

If you change your mind, let me know, or if you want I could go beat him up. Do you think that he'll actually talk to you once you get back?

Jess never fails to bring a smile to my face. I wish I could hang out with her right now. Even though I've been busy, working on the movie, it would still be nice to have a girlfriend to hang out with when I do get some free time. I guess it's just wishful thinking because I don't even have time to meet any friends. I text Jess back and hit send.

I'll let you know. I really hope that he'll talk to me… I got that impression, but who knows?

I realize, while waiting for a reply from Jess, who I could hang out with when I get some time off—Ron, the driving instructor, gave me his daughter's number and I put it in the crappy phone I'm using now. As I look at my contacts, to make sure it's still there, my phone chirps with another message from Jess.

Alright. Well, I guess waiting a couple of weeks to talk to him isn't going to kill you. You're still planning on coming back after your birthday, right? I miss my roomie.

Crap. I got so wrapped up in telling Jess about Logan that I totally forgot about telling her that I was cast in a movie and that I wasn't going back to Salem until we were done shooting.

Actually… that was the exciting news I didn't tell you because I was waiting to tell Logan first. Spencer sort of tricked me into auditioning for Dex's new movie… and I got the part. I'm the lead female and we are shooting it right now. The problem though is that I'm going to miss the start of school and I won't be back in Salem for a couple of months.

I get a response from Jess almost immediately.

OMG!!! That's so amazing! I can't believe you were holding out on me!

There's a knock on my door and it steals my attention away from my phone before I can respond to Jess. I set my phone on my pillow as I stand up and walk over to the door. Hopefully it's not my mom… there didn't seem to be anger seeping through the door. I still brace for the worst and turn the handle.

To my surprise, Dex is standing in the hall with a smile on his face when I open the door.

"Hey," he says.

"Hi."

I thought he would be in a bad mood after telling my mom… maybe by some miracle she was accepting of the fact that he cast me in his movie.

"So… your mom isn't home."

Dex looks relieved and I crack a smile.

"Where is she?"

"I have no idea, but I texted her and she said she'd be home in an hour or so."

I nod and look at him. He looks happy that he didn't have to tell her yet, but I can also see a hint of worry on his face.

"Do you want me to tell her?" I say.

He instantly shakes his head. I'm glad that he doesn't, but it didn't seem right if I didn't offer.

"No. It was my decision to cast you, so I'm going to tell her. Are you worried about how she's going to react?"

"Yeah… I have a pretty good idea of how she's going to react and I'm not looking forward to it. When she found out I didn't get into State and I tried to hide it, while I figured out a way to explain it to her, she flipped out."

Dex shakes his head, which describes my exact feeling about this entire situation. My life would be so much simpler without her in it. I'm really looking forward to the day when I never have to see her or talk to her again. I know it's awful of me to think that, but I really can't help it... not after everything she's done.

"Crazy," he says, "the whole situation is crazy. However, she reacts is going to be what it is. I'm getting myself worked up over something I have no control over."

My phone chirps and I turn around, more out of habit than anything else.

"Do you need to get that?"

"No... I'm sure it's just my friend Jess. I can text her back whenever."

"You sure?"

"Yeah, it's totally fine."

Dex pulls his phone out of his pocket and looks at it. Crap. That reminds me... I still have to tell him about the phone I broke, but I don't think this is the right time. I'll wait until things calm back down after he tells my mom about my role in the movie.

"I... I should make a call before your mom gets back."

He smiles at me and I nod. He turns and walks down the hall toward his bedroom. I slowly close the door and walk back to my bed. I'm so glad that we cleared the air last night about my mom... it makes me feel better about being around Dex. I still feel a little bad about being rude and mean to him, but I know that if I do a good job on his movie he will forgive some of that.

I pick up my phone and read the text, which is from Jess.

I've gotta go to work, but text me later if you feel like it.

I'm glad that I got a chance to catch up with her a little, it was nice. I'm really starting to miss her... even enough that I would go on a run with her. Maybe.

I pull up Jen's number on my phone, Ron's daughter, and type out a text to her.

Hey... I hope this doesn't sound weird or anything, my name is Amy and your dad gave me your phone number because I'm new in town and he said that you could show me around. If you don't have the time, don't worry about it. I just thought I would check. Hope to hear from you.

I read the text again and hit send. Most of my friends have come from school, so it's a little strange for me to do this, but I hope she replies. It's more about having some time away from the movie, to relax, than really getting to know the area—there's not really any point to that since I plan to move back to Salem as soon as we're done shooting the movie.

To my surprise, I don't have to wait long for a reply from Jen. My phone chirps as I go to set it down on my nightstand.

Hi Amy, my dad told me about you. He said you were living with Dex? That's gotta be pretty cool. I could definitely show you around town, if you want. I don't know that I'm an expert or anything, but we could hang out and go to a club or something. My schedule is pretty open right now, so just let me know when's good for you.

That's what I have no idea about… I don't know when I'll have some free time. I guess maybe I can ask him tomorrow, depending on how the talk goes with my mom tonight.

That sounds great, thanks. Work is a little hectic with me right now, but when I get a day or night off, I'll text you and let you know.

My phone chirps a few seconds later.

Sounds good.

A smile crosses my face as I set my phone down and stand up. I yawn and stretch as I head to the bathroom. I freeze mid-stride while walking back into my room. Somewhere in the house someone is yelling at the top of their lungs. I guess my mom got home and Dex is telling her right now.

I walk over to my bedroom door and unlock it, since I'm sure she'll come barging through it at any moment. I sit down on my bed and take a deep breath. Part of me wants to go out into the hallway and try to listen to what's being said, but I don't want to get caught eavesdropping and I'm sure I'll find out soon enough.

The screaming finally stops and I feel like I can breathe again. I wonder what could have happened that caused her to calm down. The only thing that comes to mind is that maybe Dex told her that there was no use in arguing because filming has already started and it's too late to do anything about it now.

My door swings open just as the anxious feeling is starting to fade. I turn and see a look of rage on her face... it's unlike anything I've ever seen before. Her eyes burn with hate and it feels like it's penetrating the deepest parts of my soul.

"You little bitch!"

She rushes toward me, pulls her right hand back, and before I can move she swings her arm and slaps my cheek. The force of the blow knocks me over and I fall off the bed. My head hits the floor and I put my hands on the back of my head in anticipation of another slap.

"Get up, right now."

I thought that I had seen my mom mad before, but this is a million times worse than when I didn't get into State. Nothing comes out of my mouth when I open it and try to scream for help.

"Get up!"

I put my hands on the floor and push myself to a kneeling position. She grabs my shirt and pulls me to my feet. A dizzy feeling fills my head and I barely stumble back onto the bed.

"How dare you? I can't believe you would do this to me."

I knew she was going to be mad, but I had no idea it would be this bad. She threatened to spank me once, many years ago, but she never did. I never imagined that she would hit me. The shock of it is almost as bad as the physical pain.

"What? You've got nothing to say for yourself?"

My cheek is still burning from the slap and my head is

25

throbbing from hitting the floor. Is this who she's become? Is this what Hollywood has made of my school teacher mom?

I watch in horror as she draws her hand back. My world slows, but there's nothing I can do about it... I can't move. Her hand crashes into my face, harder this time, and pain shoots through my body. I can feel tears starting to form in my eyes as I put my hands up to block my face.

"Say something!"

"I'm sorry."

I'm not sorry, but it's the only thing I could think to say that would stop her.

"You're sorry? You're sorry? Maybe you should have thought about the consequences before you continued to disobey me... I was already angry with you working as Dex's assistant, but you somehow thought this would be fine?"

"I don't know," I say, my words barely a whisper.

"What?"

"I don't know."

"That's your problem, Amy. You don't think. Think about how this has changed my life... I didn't want you here in the first place and now Dex cast you in his movie. Do you have any idea how bad this is? You're going to be awful and he's going to lose millions. You know that, right?"

"Dex... he said that I'm perfect for the role."

My mom huffs and walks over to the window. She crosses her arms and glares at me as she turns around. Her eyes are still filled with hate. It makes me wish I could close my eyes and disappear.

"I'm sure he did. Once again, just like with the first job he gave you, he felt obligated because you're my daughter. Come on, get real... did you actually think you could be an actress?"

I hadn't really even thought about it, but now doubt is starting to fill my head. Is she right about Dex? Would he really do that? I don't think he would, but she seems so convinced that it's hard to not agree with her.

"I don't think so," I say, "Dex wouldn't do that. You don't spend enough time around him to know how much he really cares about this movie."

The instant the words leave my lips I regret ever thinking them. The rage in her face flares up and she pulls her hand back.

"Stop it!"

She freezes. We both turn and look at Dex, who is standing in the doorframe.

"Don't tell me how to raise my daughter."

"This is my house… you don't get to physically abuse her."

My mom lets out a heavy sigh and walks toward the door. I think for a moment that she's going to slap him too, but she wouldn't dare. Dex backs out of the room and stands aside as she walks by him. She mumbles something that I can't make out, but I see the look on Dex's face and he looks furious.

Dex watches her walk down the hall toward their bedroom and then comes in my room. He sits down next to me and lifts his hand to my chin. I look away, but he turns my head toward him so he can inspect what she's done.

"Jesus."

I wince as he brushes his fingertips across my cheek. It's still throbbing and I have a feeling it's not going to stop anytime soon. I'm still in a state of shock—not like when my dad died, but it's still hard to come to terms with what just happened.

"Are you alright?"

I nod even though I'm not. I'm not alright at all.

"You sure?"

I nod again as the guilt of not telling him the truth starts to fill me. Dex stands up and walks toward the door. He turns around and forces himself to smile at me, but I can see the disdain on his face.

"Wait here… I'll be back in a few minutes."

I turn away from Dex as he walks down the hall. Even though I'm angry and upset by what my mom just did, I hope that Dex doesn't do anything he'll regret. I brace for yelling to start again, but then I hear… sirens. I've heard them a few times since I've been here, but these ones are growing louder and louder with each passing moment. The sirens abruptly spot. I wonder what it was? I assumed that this was a safe neighborhood, but maybe Dex was right about me not walking around at night.

I hold my breath, again, waiting for the yelling to commence. The doorbell rings and I freeze. Who could be here? Maybe it's a good thing… maybe this person showing up will distract Dex and my mom from fighting. I know it's only a temporary solution, but it's better than nothing.

The doorbell rings again. I walk over to my door and ease it open. I hear someone walking down the other set of steps. I guess Dex must be going to get the door. The house is quiet enough that I can hear voices, but they are muffled. They start to get clearer… it sounds like whoever is here is walking up the stairs.

"Yes… just right up here," Dex says.

I wonder who he could be talking to.

"Has this happened before?"

I wrack my brain, trying to think if I've heard his voice before, but he doesn't sound familiar.

"No," Dex says, "but she's only been living here a short time."

I really want to go out in the hall and see who it is, but I'm afraid that if I do my mom will see me. I close my door until it's open just a crack and strain to listen.

"I'm going to talk to the girl and my partner will talk to the mom."

It finally hits me… the sirens, this guy saying his partner… it had to be the police. I wonder who called them? The only thing that I can think is that maybe the neighbor heard my mom and Dex yelling. That's the only possibility.

"Sure… my room is here… and her daughter is in that room at the end of the hall."

"Thanks. If you could just wait downstairs, Sir, we will come and get you when we are done."

"Sure thing, Officer."

I close my door and release the handle slowly. I take a deep breath and stand back a few steps. The last time I spoke to the Police was when my dad died and now… now it's because of my mom.

There is a gentle knock on the door, not what I was expecting from a policeman.

"Miss, if you could please open your door… I need to talk to you."

I take another deep breath and turn the handle. I open the door and standing in front of me is a policeman whose badge identifies him as part of the LAPD.

"Do you mind if I come in?"

I nod and stand to the side. He walks a few feet into my room and turns around to look at me.

"Why don't you take a seat on the bed?"

I sit on the bed and look out the window.

"I'm Officer Brandt, my partner… Officer McElroy is talking to your mother right now. Do you want to tell me what happened?"

I clear my throat and look at him. He has kind eyes… they are hidden behind the masculine exterior of an LAPD officer, but it's obvious behind all of that he's a good guy. He takes a pen and pad of paper out of his front pocket.

"My mom… she hit me a few times. She thinks… she thinks I'm trying to mess up her life, I guess. She says that Dex only hired me and cast me because… because he felt obligated."

I look up and see him writing down everything I've said so far. He stops writing and looks at me and nods.

"That was kind of it."

"Has she ever hit you before?"

I think back… trying to remember a time when she hit me before. She has been mad plenty of times, but I don't remember her ever being as mad as tonight.

"No… she never hit me."

He looks at me for a few seconds and then goes back to writing on his pad.

"Not even a spanking?" he says, without looking up.

"Well… I mean, yeah… she spanked me a few times when I was younger, but I'm sure that I did something to deserve it."

He stops writing and looks at me for a few moments. He looks confused… and sad by what I just said. He puts his pad and pen back in his pocket and clears his throat.

"Hang tight, I'm going to go check with my partner and then I'll be back."

I nod in response. He turns and walks out of my room, leaving the door open. I sit on my bed until I see him turn down the hall toward the master and I jump up. I walk down the hall, as quietly as possible, but I hear the door to the master close. I sigh and head back to my room. I was hoping to listen to what they were saying to my mom, but no such luck.

I sigh as I sit back down on my bed and wait. I grab my phone as a distraction, and I scroll through the sparse settings, while I wait.

"Noooo!"

I look up from my phone as my mom screams.

"You can't do this!"

I stand up and walk to the door. The officers walk into the hallway on either side of my mom. Her hands are behind her back in handcuffs and she's dragging her feet. I can't believe they are arresting her… this is crazy.

"Dex! Tell them to stop!"

She looks over her shoulder at Dex as he walks into the hallway, but he doesn't respond. He just shakes his head and watches them walk down the stairs. Dex turns and walks toward the master and I hear the door close.

I wait for a few minutes... expecting Dex to come out of his room or for my mom to come back in the house, but neither happens. I eventually get up and close my bedroom door.

What a crazy twenty-four hours... and I have a feeling tomorrow is going to be a challenge.

CHAPTER FOUR

I stretch my arms and yawn as I walk down the stairs. It was nice to sleep in, it's already nine. I didn't even bother setting my alarm... I kind of figured that we wouldn't be rushing off to the set first thing in the morning.

Part of me is sad though, I would have much rather continued to work in secret... nothing about last night was pleasant. I know that it would have never worked, my mom would have found out, but I feel like it was one of those awful things that are just best to ignore.

Dex is sitting at the table in the kitchen when I walk in. I expect to see a smile on his face when he looks up at me, but it's not there... instead he looks somber. I sit down across from him as Gina walks toward the table.

"Are you hungry, Miss Amy?"

I look over at her and shake my head. The last thing I'm thinking about right now is eating.

"You should eat," Dex says, "we have a long day ahead of us."

I look over at him, but he's looking down at his phone while eating a spoonful of yogurt. Before I can protest Gina is already back in the kitchen. I guess I'm eating.

Gina returns with a plate and sets it down in front of

me. There is a slice of wheat toast, which looks buttered and has been sliced in two, two slices of crispy bacon and a scrambled egg. She also sets down a bottle of water in front of me before she goes back to doing whatever it was she was doing before I came down.

Food, which I'm usually eager to eat when Gina makes it, seems so unappetizing today. It just seems like any other food on any other day... not to mention the whole thing with my mom last night has left me in a state of shock—I still can't believe what she did and that she was arrested.

"Sorry about last night," Dex says.

I look over at him as I chew a piece of bacon. He still has that look on his face, but he's staring at his phone. I'm starting to wonder if maybe he doesn't want to look at me or something. It's a weird feeling... not something I've had from him since I got here.

"It's fine."

Dex sighs, sets his phone down and finally looks up. He still looks the same... defeated, sad... and it's hard for me to look at him. I know now that his life would have been so much better if he never showed up in Greenville. Even though he's been really nice to me, there's a part of me wishes that... that I would have never met him... and really only for his own sake.

"It's not fine. Don't pretend it is. What she did to you... it was awful. I had no idea she... I didn't think she could ever do something like that."

Before I can answer him, Dex stands up from the table and shakes his head. He takes one last look at his phone and slips it into his pocket.

"Can you be ready in twenty minutes?"

I nod and pick up a piece of toast. Dex walks out of the room, without saying anything else, and I hear him climbing the stairs by the front door. I take a sip of water to wash down the dry toast that is stuck in my throat and jump up from the table—I should have just enough time to take a quick shower.

I take a deep breath as I walk up the stairs. I'm still surprised that we're going to the set right now.

Eighteen minutes have passed by the time I shower and get back downstairs. Dex is leaning against the garage door, once again looking at his phone. He glances up at me, but doesn't make eye contact. He quickly opens the door and gets in the car. The awkward tension only gets worse once both doors of the car are closed.

I want to say something... I want to tell Dex that it's going to work out, but I'm not sure that it will. I'm not sure what's going to happen next and especially when it comes to my mom.

After a few minutes of unbearable silence, I take my phone out of my purse. I fiddle with it while Dex drives and it distracts me enough that I lose track of time and don't look up until Dex parks the car at the set.

Dex puts his hand on my shoulder as I reach for my door handle.

"We need to talk for a minute."

I nod and turn toward him. He still looks upset. I get it though... the woman he thought he loved has turned out to be a different person than who told him she was. I doubt that Dex would have asked her to come to L.A. with him if he knew this is how she would act. I still can't figure out if this is the person she has always been, but she kept it hidden away or if moving has changed her that much.

"I... I'm so sorry. I didn't know what else to do. Of course I didn't want your mom to get arrested, but I didn't know what to do. She shouldn't have hit you... that's not OK."

"I know... I just don't... I don't understand why she did it."

Dex sighs and looks out the window. I wish I could just curl up in bed and stay there forever. The last thing I want to do today is act.

"Well," he says, taking a moment to clear his throat,

"when I told her about you... being in my movie, she flipped out as you might imagine. It was a thousand times worse than what I expected. She told me that if I didn't replace you in the movie she was going to leave me... and she was going to force you to go with her."

I don't even know what to say. I can't believe that she would say that to him. The fact that we are sitting here, about to start filming for the day, speaks volumes about his decision. I'm actually a little surprised that he would choose to have me in his movie over her.

"Are you sure about this?" I say.

Dex looks at me and for the first time since yesterday I can see a semblance of happiness on his face. I hope that it's real, but I'm just not sure.

"It's the only thing I'm sure about. You're going to be in my movie and there's nothing your mom can do or say to change that."

I feel my entire body warm as I listen to his kind words. He really is such a good guy... I hope that I can make him proud and do a good job on the movie since he's gone through so much to have me in it. It's not something I think I would have been capable of a few months ago, but now I think I can do it.

"Thank you. You didn't have to do that... any of it. I really appreciate this... opportunity you've given me. You've been more kind to me than anyone and I'm going to do my best to help you make a beautiful movie."

Dex smiles at me and nods.

"Thank you, Amy. It means a lot to me that you care so much about it."

I smile at Dex and reach for the door handle. I know we've got a lot of work to do and the sooner we get it done, the better. I guess my mom will be home when we get there tonight, but I can avoid her if need be.

"I'll see you on set as soon as I'm done with hair and makeup," I say.

"Perfect. I'm going to go talk to one of the writers. I'll

see you soon."

I smile at him again as we go our separate ways. I know things haven't been easy, especially after last night, but I've really gotta remember that I've come so far in the last couple months—when I was finishing up high school in Greenville, I would have never imagined that I would be co-starring in a Hollywood film directed by Dexter Baldwin. I need to make sure that I remember that.

~~~

I close the door to my trailer and head for the couch. I plop down and let out a heavy sigh. It was a long day... much longer than I had anticipated. I kick off my shoes and put my feet up on the coffee table.

Dex told me it would be a few minutes before he was ready to leave for the night. He needed to talk to one of the writers, so I figured I would try to relax a little.

I reach for the bottle of water I left on the coffee table during one of our earlier breaks and take a long drink out of it. I lean my head back, close my eyes and wiggle until I find the perfect spot on the couch.

A knock on my door ruins my newfound relaxation.

"Yeah?"

"It's me, Spencer, can I come in?"

I sigh. It's not that I mind talking to him, but we literally just spent the entire day working together.

"Sure."

The door opens and Spencer steps in. I turn my head and look at him, but I can't reciprocate the smile on his face. It's amazing how happy he can be all of the time. I wish that I was capable of that.

"What's up?" he says.

"What do you mean?"

He sits down on the other end of the couch and turns his body toward me. I feel weird... it's not that him being here bothers me, but it's... maybe I'm afraid that if anyone finds out he was in my trailer they will think there's something between us. It seems like everyone in L.A. quickly jumps to conclusions and me being seen with Spencer has already done damage that will probably never be repaired.

"I saw it on your face all day. Every time Dex cut... the look on your face changed completely. It was like you were in a different world. Bravo on not letting that show through in your acting, that was spectacular, but it was obvious that something was truly bothering you."

I look out the window opposite of the couch. This isn't a conversation I really want to have with Spencer.

"It's fine... I'm fine."

I keep my gaze away from Spencer, but I can tell he's looking right at me... trying to figure out what it is that I'm not telling him.

"Let me know if you change your mind."

Spencer stands up and walks to the door. He turns around and I look at him finally. He's not irritated with me, but he looks saddened by the idea that I wouldn't want to talk to him about what's going on with me. He shrugs and turns to the door.

"Wait."

I notice he doesn't move his hand off the handle, but he doesn't turn it either.

"I... I just...."

I stop. All I can think about is the night Spencer took me to dinner and how guilty I felt about the whole thing. He was very kind and he listened the whole time, but it still didn't seem right. I'm sure he's got enough of his own problems that he doesn't need to hear about mine.

Spencer smiles at me as he walks back over to the couch. This time he sits next to me, in the middle of the couch. It feels funny for him to be sitting next to me, but in a good way.

"Amy... I would like to think we're friends. I thought that after the night I took you to dinner you'd feel comfortable... comfortable enough to be able to talk to me."

I nod. He's right and that's how I feel, but it still seems strange to talk to someone like Spencer about what must seem so trivial.

"I know... it's just... I don't want to trouble you... not with my stupid drama."

Spencer smiles and puts his hand on my knee. My mind tells me to pull back... that he shouldn't be touching me at all... but I don't do anything. With each passing second that his hand rests on my knee, I feel a little bit calmer. It's such a weird sensation that I'm not sure what to think of it.

"Amy, do you think I would have come to your trailer if I didn't care about what's going on with you?"

"No."

"No. I wouldn't have said anything. And then you would have continued to be upset for who knows how long."

I nod. He's right, it's probably not good for me to be in such a bad mood when I'm on set. I wonder if anyone else noticed?

"You're right."

Spencer squeezes my knee and smiles. He looks beyond happy and I can't help but smile at how excited he is that I told him he's right.

"I'm always right."

He squeezes my knee again as I roll my eyes playfully.

"Sure you are."

"So... before you get distracted by how funny I am, you should tell me what's going on with you."

I look away from Spencer and let my eyes wander the room as I try to think of exactly what to say to him. I still don't see the point of saying anything, but I have a feeling he's not going to drop it anytime soon.

"I... well... my boyfriend broke up with me...."

"Logan?"

"Yeah, Logan… so, there was that. And then… last night Dex told my mom about me being in the movie."

I pause and look at Spencer. He nods and I can tell by the look on his face that he knows telling her didn't go well.

"And when Dex told her… well, she flipped out. She came into my room and she hit me a few times and I fell on the floor… it was a pretty awful situation."

"Wow… are you hurt?"

I shake my head. My face still hurts a little, but I decide not to tell Spencer.

"No… I'm fine."

"Are you sure?"

"Yeah."

Spencer sighs and stands up. I watch as he paces up and down what I guess would be the living room of the trailer.

"But why?" he says. "Why would she hit you? Shouldn't she be happy for you? You were cast in a movie by Dexter Baldwin and you have no prior acting experience… I would say that's pretty awesome. If I had a kid and they did something like that… I would be so happy for them."

"She… she thinks that the only reason Dex cast me is because they are dating. She thinks that I'm going to be awful and ruin his movie and cost him millions in the process."

Spencer shakes his head and sits back down on the couch.

"Seriously?"

"Yeah… that's pretty much what she said to me."

"Wow. Dex cast you in his movie because you're perfect for the part. Does she know that he was resistant to it and that I had to convince him to even let you audition?"

"She doesn't care. I don't know what she thinks, but I know that she doesn't care. I think she thinks that I'm an idiot or incompetent or something… I don't know."

"Maybe if she could come to the set… and, you know, see you acting… maybe that would get her to change her mind."

"I don't think she would even bother."

"That makes me sad," he says.

I'm not sure what that even means. I look over at Spencer and he actually does look sad… not like he's about to cry sad, but he definitely looks upset. Is he really this bothered by my mom's behavior?

"Yeah?"

"Yeah… I had a mother that was so supportive of my dream of becoming an actor, so for yours to be so… so awful about the whole thing makes me sad. Every mother should support their child in whatever they choose to become. That's one of the most important things about being a parent."

I'm not even sure how to respond to that. I guess I never really thought about my mom supporting my dreams because it was always assumed that I would follow in her steps… I would go to State and then back to Greenville to be a teacher, just like her.

Now that I think about it, was that really my dream or was it what she wanted for me? Is there a difference? I have a feeling I would've been completely content with that life, but now… now I'm not so sure anymore.

"Well, that's not exactly the childhood I had growing up."

The whole conversation is starting to make me feel sad, so I take a deep breath and look out the window. This wasn't exactly where I envisioned this going… although I'm not sure what I was expecting.

"I'm sorry. That's not something I would want for anyone."

I shrug and force myself to smile. There's not much I can do about it now.

"I can tell by the look on your face that what I'm saying

isn't making it any better," he says, with a playful tone in his voice.

"It's fine... it's whatever. I'll be fine."

"What happens now? With your mom, I mean."

That's the question of the day.

"I'm not sure... she was arrested."

"Wait, what?"

He sounds shocked and I realize I didn't tell him that part of the story.

"Dex called the police, so they came and questioned us. They arrested her and that was it."

"Wow, that... that's something else. Did Dex go and bail her out?"

I shake my head, we hadn't even talked about it.

"I'm not sure what's going to happen."

"That sounds like something right out of a movie," he says.

I laugh. He's ridiculous and talking to him has definitely made me feel better. He really is a good guy—this is the second time when I've been down that he's listened to my problems and I'm glad for the opportunity to talk through it all.

"I guess he'll have to bail her out, but I don't know what happens after that... I guess things will go back to normal."

"Do you think she'll drop it and give in to the fact that you're a movie star?"

"I don't know... I really don't, but Dex told me there was no way he was going to give in to her wishes and not allow me to be in the film."

"Good, as it should be. You're magnificent and I wouldn't want to make this movie with anyone else."

I smile at Spencer. I would have never imagined my life would be like this—Spencer Thomas coming to my defense and being impressed by my acting ability. So crazy.

"Thank you so much... that's such a nice thing to say."

"It's the truth."

It's nice to feel like I'm wanted, for once. For a moment it even makes me forget about the craziness with my mom, which I guess I'll have to deal with when I get home.

I open my mouth to say something, what I'm not sure, but before I can make a fool of myself his phone chirps. Spencer takes it out of his pocket and looks down at it. A genuinely infectious smile forms on his face and he nods slightly. I wonder who could have texted him?

"Sorry," he says, as he puts his phone back in his pocket, "I've gotta get going, if you don't mind... I'm meeting someone."

"Of course not."

I do my best to smile at Spencer... it's not easy, though. I'm not sure if it's the conversation we just had or if it was the text that prompted his leaving.

"Well, I hope everything works out with your mom... and I guess I'll see you tomorrow."

"Thanks. See you tomorrow."

He smiles at me one last time and leaves my trailer. I'm glad that Spencer knocked on my door, I actually feel a lot better. I just hope that it carries over and makes tonight a little easier because I have a feeling my mom isn't going to be too happy about Dex calling the cops on her.

I sigh and try to think about something else, anything really, while I get changed back into my clothes. I put my wardrobe into the laundry bag, just like every day, and head outside. Dex is already at the car, waiting for me, and he has a grim look on his face.

CHAPTER FIVE

"What is it?" I say.

I feel panic sweeping my body as I look into his eyes. Did something happen to my mom? Dex swallows hard and gestures to the car.

"Get in."

It feels like all the air has been sucked out of my lungs. I want to ask him what happened, but he's already in the car. I hop in and Dex pulls out of the parking spot. The tension in the car dissuades me from saying anything.

"Sorry… I got a call from Gina… Ricardo bailed your mom out and she's back at the house right now."

There's panic in his voice… it's not something I've heard before. I'm not sure why he's so surprised either, I just sort of assumed that she would be at the house once we got home. Obviously that's not what Dex was thinking.

"Should she not be there?"

Dex glances over at me. He still has that same worried look on his face and now it's starting to worry me. I want to say something… anything really, that might change his mood, but I'm scared—I haven't seen this side of Dex and I don't know what to do.

"She… I don't know. I… I'm not sure that I feel, but I

do know that I don't want her in *my* house when I'm not there. There's no telling what she could do."

That's definitely not what I was expecting Dex to say. Just a few days ago he was fine with taking care of her and paying for everything and now… now he didn't even want her alone in his house. I know that I'm at fault for endangering their relationship, which is exactly what my mom said would happen.

I know she's going to let me know that as soon as I see her and I'm dreading it.

"I'm not sure what to do," he says.

I wait for a minute to see if he's going to say something else, but he turns his attention back to the road.

"What do you mean?" I say, finally breaking the silence when we are halfway home.

"I… I'm not sure, really. I think I'm in love with her… but after last night… I never thought I would see something like that as long as I lived. I'm really so sorry about that, Amy, I really am."

"It's OK… it was her, she's the one who went crazy."

Dex sighs and glances over at me for a brief second.

"But I'm the one who chose to cast you in my film… you never asked for that."

He shakes his head and comes to a stop in front of the gate. He sighs as it slowly opens and he pulls the car through. He turns off the ignition once we are inside the garage, but instead of getting out he turns to me.

"When we go inside, you should stay behind me… I don't want her to direct any more of her anger and animosity toward you."

"Are you sure?"

"Yes… because if she even tries to hit you again, I will make sure that she wishes she had never met me."

I nod. There's a part of me that wonders what that means…. I have a pretty good idea, but I wonder if he would really have her arrested again. I'm not sure what that would really do, however, the sound of his voice suggested something a little more... permanent. The last thing I need is her being pissed at me for the rest of her life because this whole thing is somehow my fault.

"Alright?" he says.

"Yes."

We get out of the car and walk over to the door that leads inside. Dex closes his eyes for a brief moment. He takes a deep breath, opens the door and I follow him through.

Before we take more than three steps into the house, Gina rushes up to us with a crazed look on her face.

"Mr. Baldwin, she's... crazy."

Her voice is unsteady and it's obvious that whatever my mom has been doing is making Gina uneasy.

"What's happening?"

Dex is suddenly calm and his words come easily. I wonder what happened to the massive amount of stress he was feeling just moments ago... maybe talking about it helped or maybe he knows how worried Gina is and feels the need to take control of the situation.

"She... she is slamming doors and I hear things breaking, but I'm afraid to go up there, Mr. Baldwin."

"Gina, it's fine... why don't you head home for the night? We can fend for ourselves for dinner."

"Are you sure?"

Her voice is still a little shaky. I have a feeling, based on the looks she has on her face, that my mom probably said something to her that sent her into this state of shock and fear.

"Yes, of course."

"Thank you Mr. Baldwin... I'll see you tomorrow."

Dex nods and smiles at her. It was a nice thing to do, but I'm starting to expect that kind of behavior from him... he really is a nice guy. It makes it that much harder to wonder why he likes my mom, especially after her recent behavior. I feel bad... she doesn't deserve him and he doesn't deserve to be with someone like her.

Gina smiles at us, turns and walks back into the kitchen.

"You ready?" he says.

"I guess?"

Dex lets out a little chuckle and heads toward the stairs. I'm as ready as I'm ever going to be. The day when I no longer have to be afraid of her is going to be amazing. I just don't know how or when that's going to happen. It's weird though, the feeling of wishing I had never come here is starting to fade—I'm still upset about what happened to my relationship with Logan because of it... at the same time I'm excited about the movie and everything that goes with it.

"I was hoping for a little more conviction than that."

I look over at Dex, but the smile on his face tells me he was just joking.

"What? You don't think I'm funny?" he says.

I just shake my head and roll my eyes. He is funny... I would laugh if we were about to do anything other than talk to my mom.

He smiles at me, turns and heads up the stairs. I take a deep breath and follow him. We both freeze halfway up when we hear a loud crash followed by screaming. He shakes his head and starts walking again. I can't believe how crazy she's acting... this isn't the same woman who raised me... she's changed forever.

We turn toward the noise, which is coming from the master suite, when we reach the top of the stairs. There's more screaming followed by another crash, but this time it doesn't even slow Dex down. I cringe as I wonder what she's breaking and how expensive it is. I have no idea how Dex is seemingly so calm right now, I would be furious if I were him.

I hold my breath as we turn right and head down the hall toward the master. The door is open and I see my mom rush by with a suitcase in her hands. It suddenly makes things much more clear. Is she really going to just pack up and leave this all behind? I can't imagine that she would... what would she do? Go back to Greenville? I really doubt it. If I had to guess, she's probably trying to make Dex feel bad and make sure that he insists she stay. I'm not sure what Dex is going to do, but I guess it doesn't matter because this is his house. If it were up to me, I would ask her to leave and never come back.

Dex slows for a moment and glances over his shoulder at me. I can tell by the look in his eyes that he wants me to stay in the hallway—he's afraid that it could get messy and he doesn't want her to hit me, again. I nod and stop in my tracks. Dex disappears into the master suite and closes the door.

I take a deep breath and mentally prepare myself for what's about to happen. I look down at my hands as they start to shake. Who lives like this? Even with all the great opportunities Dex has given me, I wish I could be back in my old life... where my parents were still together and I visited them in Greenville on the weekends. I feel so far removed from that life... it almost feels like it wasn't me.

"What do you want?" she says.

My mom yelling pulls me out of my near dream state and back to reality.

"This is my house," Dex says.

She screams again.

"So?"

"So... so... I'm not going to let you act like this, in my house."

"That's why I'm leaving!"

Dex doesn't respond... I think about what he said earlier, but I somehow still expected that he would try and stop her.

"What... is that what you want? You want me to leave?"

He doesn't answer her, but I hear what sounds like glass shattering.

"Stop breaking my things," he says, in a calm tone.

I don't know how he can be so calm, unless he's just acting that way... but I doubt it. I would be screaming right back at her, if I were Dex. I guess I should give him some credit because she doesn't respond by yelling... instead she's silent.

The door to the room swings open and Dex walks toward me. He doesn't have a panicked or worried look on his face... instead he just looks... he looks peaceful.

"What?" I say.

"I think you better go to your room... I have a feeling this is going to get out of hand rather quickly."

I wrinkle my brow... I want to stay and listen. I want to find out what's going to happen, but I can tell by the look on his face that he's not going to let me stay. I don't think that he doesn't want me to hear what they're saying... it's more than that, like he thinks she might do something like she did last night and he wants to protect me from that.

"OK."

I force half a smile on my face as I turn around, slump my shoulders and head toward my bedroom.

"What are you telling her?" she says.

I resist the temptation to turn around and keep walking toward my room. I do slow down a little, just so I can hear what they are saying while I walk.

"What do you mean?"

"What did you say to her?" she says.

"That's none of your business."

I hear glass shatter and I stop. I know I should keep going... I know I should go into my room and lock the door, but I can't help myself.

"It is my business! She's my daughter!"

"You don't get it, do you?"

She breaks something else, not glass... but it still shatters. I cringe at the thought of the sheer amount of monetary damage she's causing to his things—it'll probably amount to more than I'll earn in my entire life.

"You're so stupid," she says, "Amy is still seventeen... not for much longer, but that doesn't matter."

It's quiet for a moment. I realize what she's saying... and I want to run back down that hall, but I'm going to follow his wishes. She... she's telling him that if she walks out of here, and leaves him, she's going to force me to go with her.

I want to scream. There's no way I'm letting her take me. She got me to leave Logan, to come here, but now... now I'm not leaving here until the movie is done.

"Don't do this... I need her... and she wants to be in my movie."

My mom laughs... a sick, twisted laugh. That's exactly what she wants to do. I have a feeling that it's what she's been planning from the moment she was taken away in handcuffs. She knew she wasn't going to stay with Dex, not after he had her arrested... so she decided to do what would hurt him the most and that was taking me away.

"And this is why you should have listened to me and fired her."

"You can't make her leave," Dex says.

"Yes... Yes, I can. Until she turns eighteen, I can do whatever I want."

She can try, but there's no way I'm leaving... not this time.

"I will never forgive you, if you do this."

"Ha! I'll never forgive you for having me arrested!"

"What did you expect me to do?"

"I expected you to listen to me about Amy and I expected you to take my side. I'm leaving and I'm taking her with me and there's nothing you can do or say to change my mind."

I do the only thing I can think of.

I grab my purse and run.

CHAPTER SIX

I look over my shoulder at the front door as the gate starts to open. My whole body is shaking as adrenaline starts to course through me. I need to get out of here before she notices. I turn sideways and slip through the gate. I don't dare look back as the house fades into the distance.

My muscles scream for a break and I give in as I reach Santa Monica Boulevard. It's not very far, but I'm not wearing running shoes and I didn't stretch. I'm sure it doesn't help that I haven't been running, or even swimming, but I've been eating plenty.

I spot an empty bench just a few feet away and sit down. I take my phone out of my purse, for a distraction, while I catch my breath.

I really don't know what to do—if my mom finds me she's going to make me go back to Greenville with her. There's not really any way Dex can stop her. I start to cry as I feel my world crashing down around me... again.

I'm really starting to wonder if things will ever get better.

As I put my hands on the bench to stand up, my phone starts to ring. I freeze and listen, thinking that I must be hearing things. It rings a second time and I open my purse to fish it out. My heart skips a beat as I wonder if maybe, just maybe, it's Logan calling me.

I'm disappointed when I see it's Jess... which really isn't fair to her. I'm not sure why I thought Logan would call me, it makes much more sense for it to be her.

"Hey," I say.

"Hey... are you alright?"

The tears start to flow again.

"No... not really."

"What's wrong?"

Her voice is as soft and sweet as ever. I wish I could see her right now, I know she would make me feel better.

"Amy? Are you still there?"

"Yeah...."

I force myself to stop crying and I dry my eyes with my shirt.

"Are you safe?"

It's an interesting question. I don't exactly feel safe after last night, but I know that Dex is watching out for me.

"Amy?"

"Sorry... yeah, I think I'm safe."

"You *think* you're safe?"

"Well... I ran out of the house and I'm down on Santa Monica Boulevard."

"What happened?"

"My mom... she's crazy."

"Amy, take a deep breath."

I pull the phone away from my ear, close my eyes and take two deep breaths. My body and mind start to calm down and I put my phone back to my ear as I open my eyes.

"Now," Jess says, "tell me what happened... just take your time."

I take another deep breath as I ready myself to tell her what happened.

For ten minutes I talk and Jess doesn't say a word,

which surprises me about as much as what happened.

"And then I ran out... and then you called," I say.

"Wow, you're right... she's totally crazy."

I let a laugh slip through my lips, not because today has been funny... but I don't know what else to do. I look into the sky... the sky that should be filled with stars like in Greenville, but there are so many lights that I can't see a thing. It makes me kind of sad, just another thing I miss about home.

"So," Jess says, "what are you going to do now?"

That's the real question. Can I really go back to Greenville or Salem? I don't want to give this up. I know that it's a crazy dream, being in a Hollywood movie and that at *some point* I'll have to let go and live in reality, but I was hoping to finish the movie first.

"I... I don't know. I feel like if I go back to the house, she's either going to be there waiting for me or the cops will be. It's like she's going to stop me no matter what. Just thinking about it makes me feel sick."

There's silence from the other end of the line. I look at my phone, but it is still showing the call as being connected.

"Jess?"

"One sec... I'm trying to figure out what you should do."

Normally I'm not a huge fan of someone telling me what I should do, but I'm anxious to hear if she can think of something... anything.

I feel like every second where she doesn't speak is making the chance of her thinking of something less and less.

"I've got it," she says.

A faint smile forms on my face. I really hope she has a good idea.

"You need to call Spencer and see if you can stay with him. It sounds like your mom is going to leave Dex and if she can't find you... well, then she can't make you go with her."

I cringe at her suggestion as I think about what would happen if the paparazzi saw me going into his house and not coming out until the next morning. I know it's unlikely, but I don't like the idea of it.

"I dunno… what if someone found out?"

"What do you mean?"

"Well, what… what if someone saw me go into his house?"

"You could stay in a hotel for a few days."

I wish I could, but I don't really have any money.

"I'm not getting paid until we are done filming, so I can't do that either."

I feel tears forming in the corner of my eyes. I lift the phone away from my ear as I take a deep breath and try to calm myself down.

"Look," she says, her voice sounding stern, "go to Spencer's, it's the best option and I'm sure he'll let you stay there."

"Do you think so?"

"He'd better. Give me his phone number and if he doesn't I'll give him a piece of my mind."

I forgot until now that his number was in the phone I broke. I have no way of calling him or Dex.

"I just realized… I broke my phone that had his number. There's no way for me to get a hold of him."

"What about Dex? Can you call him and ask for Spencer's number?"

"No, I don't have his number."

I want to kick myself for not telling Dex about the phone when I had the chance. I really was trying to avoid making him mad, but now… now I wish I would've.

"Hmm… let me think."

I feel so worthless… like I can't do anything right.

I'm starting to feel as if maybe I should give up… like I should give in and go back to Greenville. I don't know how much longer I can keep up this constant struggle to balance everything. It's not even about making my mom happy, I don't care about that… I just want her to leave me alone, but I feel like that's never going to happen while I'm still seventeen.

"What if you just show up at Spencer's house?"

I wrinkle my brow… that would be fine, and the thought had already crossed my mind, but I have no idea where he lives.

"I don't know where he lives… I've never been to his house."

I look up as a woman sits down on the bench next to me. I force myself to smile as our eyes meet, but she doesn't smile back… instead she frowns at me and then looks down at her phone. I roll my eyes and turn my attention back to the phone call.

"One second," Jess says.

I glance back at the woman next to me, out of the corner of my eye, and now she's staring at me. A weird noise in the background of my call with Jess distracts me from the weird lady.

"What is that?" I say.

"Oh… I'm… sorry, I'm typing."

"You're typing?"

"Yeah… I'm trying to find Spencer's house."

"What do you mean?"

There's a pause and I hear her typing again.

"I'm searching for it on the Internet… he's famous… so there's a good chance that his house will be shown in a picture or something."

I'm glad I'm on the phone with Jess because I would have never thought of that… it's actually really clever.

"Did you find anything?"

"Not yet… wait, I found it!"

The excited tone of her voice puts a smile on my face—a real one.

"Now what?"

"I'll text you his address."

My phone chirps a second later and I look down to see the text from her. It's his address, which I obviously don't recognize, but I remember seeing the road a few times, Alpine Dr., and it's not very far away. I put my phone back up to my ear.

"Got it... and I actually know where it is... well, I sort of know where it is."

"Yay!"

I almost laugh at the sheer ridiculousness of Jess. I wish I could hug her right now.

"Thank you, so much... really, it means more than you know."

"Of course... and don't worry, you can make it up to me when you actually come back to Salem one of these days."

The tone of her voice is kind... she doesn't want me to go to Salem until I'm ready, which is nice to hear after dealing with my mom and Logan.

"Whatever you say."

"I should get going... I've got work in like... twenty minutes and you've gotta go find Spencer."

"Thanks again."

"Don't mention it... be safe and don't do anything I wouldn't do."

I smile as Jess ends the call before I can say anything else. I put my phone in my pocket as I stand up and try to figure out which direction I should be heading.

"Excuse me, Miss?"

I turn toward the strange woman who is sitting on the bench. The look on her face has completely changed and now it looks like she's genuinely interested in me.

"Yes?"

"I'm sorry to bother you... but are you on TV or something?"

Great, just what I need... another person who recognizes me from a tiny segment on TV. The funny thing is that this woman would never have known who I was... but now... now she's probably going to tell all of her friends how she ran into a "celebrity" on the street.

"No... sorry, I'm just me."

She frowns as a look of disappointment crosses her face. Hopefully she's not irritated with me, but I don't feel the need to remind her of why she recognizes me. Being recognized by strangers is something that I'm definitely not going to miss once I move back.

I turn away and start walking down the sidewalk, in what I am fairly certain is the right direction. If it's not, I'll be able to tell in the next few minutes.

After twenty minutes, and a few blocks, my phone chirps. I take it out of my pocket and read the text from Jess.

Are you there yet? Is it really nice?

I smile and sit down on a concrete wall next to the sidewalk. It feels good to rest my feet... running from the house didn't help after standing the better part of the day in shoes with a thin sole and I would like nothing more than to take a hot bath, but that's not going to happen anytime soon.

No, I'm still walking... haven't found the road yet, but I think it's not that much further.

I lift my right foot off the ground and move my ankle in a circle and then do the same with my left foot. Hopefully it will help and I won't have to stop again.

Poo. Well, text me later or something... I'm at work now, but I'll check my phone when I get home.

Sounds good.

I put my phone back in my pocket and stand up. Unfortunately, my feet don't feel any better. I sigh and start walking again, since it's really my only option at this point. I guess I could take a cab, but I don't really want to spend what little money I have left. I don't really need it for anything in particular, but one never knows.

After another five minutes of walking I finally see the sign for Alpine Drive at the next intersection. A happy feeling starts to creep through my body, which, given what's happened in the last twenty-four hours is pretty surprising. Am I excited to see Spencer? No... that can't possibly be it. It must be the fact that he can help me in some way to avoid leaving to go back to Greenville.

It seems weird to want to stay here... it's amazing how quickly things change.

I look down Alpine Drive and I can see the numbers on the first two houses. They're going down, which means I'm heading in the right direction. I start walking and it seems like in just moments I'm away from the businesses that line Santa Monica Boulevard and I'm already in a full-on residential area.

Five minutes of walking later, and crossing a few smaller streets, I stop in front of his house. It's starting to get dark and there aren't any street lights, so I'm glad that I made it. A light above the front door is on... so I guess he is home. I walk up the stone paved walkway and take a deep breath before ringing the doorbell.

It's a really nice house, but not as large as Dex's. There are two pillars, one on either side of the door, a few feet from the end of the walkway. The door is a dark wood that looks very old and worn, but quite solid. Even though it's not as nice or as large as Dex's house, it's still beautiful and fits in with the other houses in the area. I wish I could live in a house like this someday... but I know that's never going to happen. A girl can dream though, right?

I try to think of what to say to Spencer... it's kind of awkward to just show up at his house, but I didn't see any other option. I can hear the bell ringing inside and I take a step back. The door swings open, but it's not Spencer standing in front of me... it's... it's a woman who looks oddly familiar.

"Did you not see the sign?" she says.

"What?"

She points to a sign in the small window next to the door. It's a white sign with black letters that say 'No

Soliciting'. She closes the door before I even turn my head back in her direction.

My face turns red as I step back onto the walkway and head toward the sidewalk. Spencer must have moved or maybe this was never his house, but either way I feel embarrassed about disturbing that woman.

I'm not sure what to do now... I can't call Jess and I'm not going to call Logan. I sigh and try to mentally prepare myself for whatever comes next.

CHAPTER SEVEN

"Amy!"

I turn around and see Spencer jogging down the walkway toward me. He has a goofy grin on his face and I can see the woman standing in the doorway. The look on her face makes it fairly clear that she is irritated and angry that he rushed over to stop me.

"It's good to see you," he says.

Spencer puts his arms around me and gives me a strong hug. I halfway wrap my arms around him, not wanting to give him the wrong idea… but it actually feels good to be in his arms. I can't really explain it, but I feel safe and even though the hug lasts only seconds the feeling doesn't fade.

"You too."

"What are you doing here? Did Dex drop you off?"

I shake my head as tears start to fill my eyes.

"What's wrong?" he says.

"My mom… she…."

I can't hold the tears back any longer and I cover my face as I cry.

"Shhh… it's going to be OK," he says.

Spencer puts his arms around me and I push my face against his shoulder. He pats me on the back.

"Let's go inside and you can tell me about it."

I nod as he lets me go and I follow him to the front door. The woman is still standing in the door and she doesn't look like she's about to move.

"Monica, maybe you can come back tomorrow?"

That's where I recognize her from… she's Monica Lister, the woman who they showed with Spencer on that TV show… his ex-girlfriend. I wonder if they are getting back together and that's why she's here?

"Seriously? Are you kidding me, Spencer?"

"Monica…."

"Ugh, fine… whatever."

She walks back into the house and I follow Spencer inside. Monica picks up a purse from a table in the hallway and glares at me before walking out of the door. She doesn't say another word to me or Spencer and slams the door on her way out.

"Don't mind her… she's… whatever, it doesn't matter."

I stop and look at a painting on the wall. It's beautiful, unlike anything I've ever seen. It has a modern feel to it, but at the same time it reminds me of a time long gone. The painting is of a woman, sitting on a park bench, and she's holding a worn doll, which is missing an arm, in her hands and tears are rolling down her face. There's so much sadness for such a beautiful painting.

"Are you coming?"

I turn and look at Spencer. He's standing near the end of the entryway, with a smile on his face.

"It's beautiful," I say, as I point at the painting.

"Thank you… my mother painted that when she was young."

He nods toward the interior of the house, so I turn and walk toward him.

"Is she an artist? Your mom?"

"No, she was a nurse, but she painted for fun."

We walk into a massive room that has a kitchen, a

living room and a dining room. I've never seen a house with this kind of layout before and I really like it.

"Whatcha think?"

"It's cool… I've never seen a house like this."

Spencer laughs and walks over to one of the modern looking couches in the middle of the room. He plops himself down and puts his feet up on the glass coffee table in front of him.

"Thanks. It's an open floor plan… it's great for parties and stuff. I like it."

I nod as I walk over to the couch. I sit down on the other end and turn my body toward him. He smiles at me, takes his feet off the coffee table and turns toward me.

"So… what's going on?"

"Well… I told you about last night…."

"Did Dex go and get your mom?"

I shake my head and look out the large window behind Spencer. The yard looks perfect, just like everything else in L.A., and I can see a pool. It's not as big as the one in Dex's house, but it's still a pretty good size. I turn my attention back to Spencer, I don't want my distraction to come across as disinterest in our conversation.

"No… Ricardo actually went and bailed her out. She was at the house when we got home and she was… breaking things in the house and she pulled out a suitcase."

"Wow… that's crazy. I'm not even sure what to say to that."

"Yeah, she's pretty much out of her mind."

"So you left and came here?"

"I… I wasn't sure where else to go. She said she was going to take me away, tonight, and I wouldn't be able to be in the movie."

"I'm… I'm so sorry, Amy, that's really crappy."

"Yeah… so I freaked out and… and I just ran out of the house."

I force myself not to cry even though it's what I really want.

"Well, I'm glad that you came here. How did you find my house?"

"My friend in Salem, Jess, she found it on the Internet and I walked here."

A look of surprise crosses his face, but it quickly fades and is replaced by a smile.

"I hope you don't mind," I say, "I just didn't know where else to go."

Spencer hops up from the couch and walks toward the kitchen area.

"Of course not, I don't mind at all. Can I get you a drink?"

"Water would be great."

Spencer opens the fridge, takes out two bottles of water and comes back to the couch. He hands me a bottle and then opens his as he sits down.

"Actually, I'm glad you showed up."

"Yeah? Why?"

Spencer takes a drink of his water.

"So does Dex know you were heading here?"

He doesn't answer my question, but I have a feeling it had to do with Monica being here when I showed up and I decide not to press him.

"No… I broke my phone that had his number in it."

"How did you call your friend?"

I take my crappy phone out of my pocket and hold it up.

"Let me see it," he says.

I hand him my phone and he bites his lip as he quickly punches keys. He hands the phone back to me and winks.

"I put his number in your phone… and mine, too. You can always call me if you're in trouble and then you won't have to walk here."

"Thanks."

I put my phone back in my pocket and take a drink of water. Spencer shifts on the couch, takes his phone out of his pocket and looks at it for a brief moment before putting it on the coffee table.

"So... what are you going to do about your mom?"

"I... I'm not really sure, but I don't want to leave... there's no way I can leave. I feel like Dex really went out on a limb to cast me in the movie and I want to do a good job."

"Good... I hate that you're not listening to your mom, but I agree with you... you're the only one who can make this film work and there's no way I'm letting her take you away."

I smile at Spencer, but the look on his face instantly tells me he's not trying to be funny. I quickly look away and let my eyes wander the room.

"I guess I should text Dex and tell him where I am," I say.

I take out my phone and text him.

Hey, Dex, I'm at Spencer's. I didn't know where else to go. Amy.

I stare at my phone for a few seconds, expecting a reply to appear. I eventually put my phone away and turn my attention back to Spencer.

"Do you think your mom is actually going to just leave without you?" he says.

I hadn't really thought the whole thing through and he brings up a good point... what exactly did I expect to achieve by leaving Dex's? I doubt the sheer amount of anger in her would allow me to just be free.

"I... I don't know."

I close my eyes and take a deep breath. I just want things to be easy... for once. I thought that's the direction things were heading, once I met Logan, but now... now I feel like I've lost all my faith and I'm starting to think things might never get better. Is this the life I'm destined to live? Am I really going to spend the rest of my life bending to the wishes of my mom? I know that I'll be free of her once I turn eighteen, but I have a feeling she's not going to let me go that easy.

"If you want, you could stay here... at least until your mom leaves town or gives up or until your birthday."

My eyes grow wide as each word leaves his mouth. I had really only hoped that he would let me crash on his couch, or something, for the night... I certainly wasn't expecting this.

"Are you sure?"

He smiles at me and stands up from the couch.

"Of course."

"Thank you... I really appreciate it."

Spencer waves his hand at me and walks toward the fridge.

"It's all good... there's no way I'm letting you go, we've gotta finish this film."

I smile at Spencer, stand up and walk into the kitchen area. He turns back to the fridge and I find my mind wandering. I wonder why he's so insistent on having me be a part of this film? I get that Dex has a lot on the line, but it shouldn't really matter to Spencer... not in the same way at least.

"Thanks," I say.

"Are you hungry?"

My stomach grumbles, but I don't think it was loud enough for Spencer to hear. I already feel bad enough about imposing on him and staying here tonight that I don't want to bother him anymore.

"No... I'm fine."

Spencer turns around and looks at me with an inquisitive look on his face.

"So," he says, "you're hungry, but you feel bad about this... all of this?"

I blink a few times as I try to process the fact that he said almost exactly what I was thinking. Spencer laughs, shakes his head and turns back to the fridge.

"It will never be said that I, Spencer Thomas, has guests and lets them go hungry."

I can't help but smile. He's a funny guy and I'm actually

starting to feel normal again after everything that happened earlier… well, I'm feeling as close to normal as is possible. For a brief moment I feel like I'm actually able to forget about my mom. I know it's not going to last, but I try to savor it while it does.

"So… are you hungry?"

"Yes," I say, finally giving in.

Spencer looks over his shoulder and flashes me a quick smile. By the time I smile back, he's already pulling stuff out of the fridge. I walk into the kitchen and lean against the center island. Apparently satisfied with the pile of food on the island, he closes the fridge and smiles at me.

"Do you ever cook?" he says.

I'm not sure if he's serious and the only response I can think of is a nervous laugh. I can feel my face turning red as he smiles at me.

"Well?"

"I… no, not really."

I don't feel like admitting that I never really learned to cook. My mom always did the cooking back in Greenville and Gina has been making the food here… not to mention it seems like we eat out almost every day. It's almost like I feel ashamed of it or something, which sounds stupid enough by itself.

"I like to think of myself as a decent cook… I'm not like a professional or anything, but I make some pretty good meals that everyone seems to like."

I can detect a certain level of confidence in his voice, which isn't unusual since there usually is a trace of it… but now it seems more obvious, almost like he really is good enough to be a professional. It's a weird combination… it's like he's confident but at the same time humble.

"I was thinking we could make a salad and some pasta, how does that sound?"

My stomach grumbles again and I can tell by the smile on Spencer's face that he heard it this time.

"It sounds good."

He opens a drawer on the island and takes out two large knives. He puts one in front of me and walks over to a cupboard near the sink. Spencer takes out two plastic cutting boards, one red and one white, and walks back to the island. He sets the white one down in front of me and places the red one in front of him.

"There... now," he says, "you can cut the lettuce and onion."

He pushes a red onion and a head of lettuce toward me. He grabs something that's wrapped in foil and starts to open it. Spencer takes two beets, that look cooked already, out of the foil and he starts to pull the skin off. He looks up at me while doing it and smiles.

"First, cut the ends off the onion and make a shallow cut into it so you can peel the skin off."

I pick up the knife and take a deep breath. It looks quite dangerous and my only hope is that I come out of this unscathed. I carefully cut the ends off and then make the slit, just like Spencer told me to. I feel relieved to set down the knife and peel the onion. My eyes start to burn after two seconds and I'm forced to put the onion down and take a step back.

"You OK?"

I nod my head as I close my eyes and try to stop them from watering.

"Come over here," Spencer says.

I open my left eye just enough to watch him walk over to the fridge. He nods toward it and I manage to make my way around the island and to him without smashing into anything. I've cut an onion before, but it didn't have this kind of effect on me.

"Wow... my eyes are like on fire."

Spencer lets a little chuckle slip through his teeth. I shoot him a glare and he stops.

"Sorry," he says.

I shrug and reach my hand toward my face... I feel like rubbing my eyes will relieve some of the burning.

"No, don't touch your eyes... that will only make it that much worse."

His voice is stern, but not mean sounding, and I lower my hand and walk toward him. As I reach him, Spencer takes my hand in his. It's warm, but not sweaty or anything and I already feel like I'm calming down. I hear a door open, that's either the fridge or freezer, but I don't open my eyes.

"Here, lean forward and open your eyes."

I feel his other hand move to the low of my back... and normally I would react or at least ask him to move it, but my eyes are burning so bad that I can't think of anything else right now. As I lean forward, a blast of cold air slams into my face. I'm not sure why Spencer is having me put my head in the freezer....

"Open your eyes as wide as you can."

I doubt this is going to help, but I guess I might as well humor him. I open my eyes and it feels like icicles are stinging my eyes and for a moment it's worse than before... but then... then the burning starts to fade and within a few seconds it's gone completely. I blink a few times, just to make sure that the burning is really gone before I take my head out of the freezer.

"That... that's amazing," I say.

Spencer smiles at me and turns away. I close the freezer and watch as he opens a drawer on the far end of the kitchen. I head back to the island and pick up my knife to finish chopping the onions.

"Wait."

Spencer extends a piece of wrapped gum to me. I wrinkle my brow and tilt my head to the side. What could the gum possibly be for?

"Just chew it."

I unwrap the gum and look around the kitchen for a trash can to throw the wrapper.

"Where's the trash?"

"I'll take it."

I hand the wrapper to Spencer, who walks over to the sink and opens the cupboard under it. He turns back to me and flashes me another smile.

"It'll help with the onions… just chew it while you cut them and they won't make your eyes water as much."

I pop the gum in my mouth and start to chew. It's a funny little trick and I do hope that it works because I don't want to keep walking over to the freezer every thirty seconds. I pick up my knife again and stare down the onion.

"How do you want this cut?" I say.

"Just in thin sort of strips."

I nod and cut the onion once and hold it out for him to see.

"Perfect," he says.

I cut the rest of the onion and to my surprise it doesn't burn my eyes at all. It's actually kind of amazing… the gum trick really works.

Once I finish cutting the onions, I look up at Spencer and watch as he slices the beets into perfect cubes. A smile forms on my face as I watch him become totally consumed with the simple task. It's actually kind of cute. As the thoughts form in my head, I quickly push them out and wonder what Monica was doing here… I wish that I could ask Spencer, I really am curious, but I know it's not any of my business.

"What?" Spencer says, without moving his eyes from his cutting.

"Huh?"

"Did you need something?"

My face turns red as I realize that Spencer noticed me staring at him. Hopefully he just noticed and didn't notice the sheer amount of time that I was standing there… just looking at him. It was innocent, but still….

"Yeah… I… what should I do now?"

Spencer slowly slides his knife as he makes the last cut into the dark red beet. He pushes the cutting board away from himself and looks up at me with that smile on his face… the one that melts the hearts of every girl under the age of twenty, and some of their moms, and… and I force myself to look away.

CHAPTER EIGHT

I gently push my nearly empty plate away from myself. The food was amazing, magnificent really, but I can't eat another bite.

"Are you sure you don't want some more pasta?" Spencer says.

"I can't... it was really good, but I'm so full."

Spencer smiles as he reaches for the bowl of pasta and fills up his plate a third time. He must really work out a lot if he can eat that much food and stay in such good shape... not that I'm about to ask him.

"That... that was a really wonderful dinner... thank you." I say.

Spencer pushes the bowl back into the center of the table and smiles at me. He picks up his fork, thrusts it into the pile of pasta and starts to twirl it as he looks up at me.

"Thank you... you helped make it."

I smile at him... it's true, I did help, but I feel like he did most of it... not to mention he was essentially coaching me the entire time. It was fun though, not that I would ever really admit it. I'm not even sure what made it fun because my idea of fun is definitely not cooking. Maybe it had to do with Spencer being the one in charge.

"I'm not sure how much I really helped," I say.

Spencer finishes the bite of pasta and sets down his fork.

"You helped plenty, trust me."

I smile and tilt my head a little... I really don't think that I did, but if he's going to insist, I'm not going to argue with him.

"Really," he says, "Monica never... never mind."

Spencer looks down at his plate and reaches for his fork, but then he pushes his plate away and stands up from the table. I can feel my brow wrinkle as I wonder what it was that changed his demeanor so quickly.

"What... what's wrong?"

Spencer shakes his head, reaches across the table and takes my plate. He turns and walks toward the kitchen without looking at me. I stand up from the table and follow him. He puts the dishes in the sink and turns on the faucet. I lean against the counter, a few feet away from him, and lean to the side to try and get a look at his face.

"Nothing, I'm fine."

Spencer turns the water off and turns toward me with a smile on his face. Did I imagine the change in his mood? I shrug and force myself to smile back at him. I could have sworn that as soon as he brought up Monica there was a shift in how he was acting... like it made him sad or something.

I reach into my pocket and pull out my phone and check to see if Dex has responded yet. There's still nothing from him and I'm starting to wonder if my mom is still there... or... I hate to even think it, but I know she's capable of doing something drastic and I'm starting to worry about Dex a little. I hope that he's alright.

"Anything from Dex?" Spencer says.

I shake my head as I push my phone back into my pocket.

"I'm starting to worry," I say.

Spencer nods and leans against the counter. He looks

concerned, but I'm not sure if it's about Dex or about Monica.

"Well," he says, "I guess there isn't much we can do right now… not until you hear from Dex. I'll try texting him, too."

Spencer takes his phone out of his pocket, a new looking Smartphone of course, and his thumbs dance on the screen for just a few moments before he puts his phone back.

"I just told him that you were here and that if we didn't hear from him that you would be spending the night."

"Thanks."

Spencer opens his mouth… and shuts it without saying anything. I would swear, by the look on his face that he has something that he really wants to tell me. I just smile at him and decide not to press him, not after he's been kind enough to let me stay here.

"So," Spencer says, "are you looking forward to the publicity tour?"

"The what?"

"The publicity tour… for the movie."

I try to think if Dex mentioned it before, but it's not ringing any bells.

"I… I don't know what you're talking about."

The surprised look on his face fades and is replaced by a smile. He nods his head toward the living room and I follow him to the couch. We each take an end and turn toward each other.

"Well… usually for a film, even a low budget one like this, there will be a publicity tour where the actors and the director go around and do interviews and go to premiers and that kind of stuff."

"That makes sense. When is that?"

"Usually it's not for a few months after filming… when the editing and post-production are all done."

I nod. That makes sense. Hopefully it won't be that long after we're done because I don't want to miss any more school than my first semester. I guess I need to talk to Dex about it next time I see him... well, maybe once things are settled.

"I guess I'm excited...."

Spencer laughs and smiles at me.

"I was really excited for the publicity tour on my first film... it was called Dangerous Fury. I'm sure you've never seen it... no one really has. I had a small part, but the director thought it would be worth having me on the publicity tour."

It's cute how his face just lights up when he talks about being an actor. It must be an amazing feeling to have that kind of passion about your work... I hope that someday I feel that about something. I certainly haven't felt that way about any of the jobs I've had so far and I'm still not sure about this acting thing... it's been fun, but I don't know that it would ever be a permanent thing, even if that's what I wanted.

"So, it's going to be a few months after we finish shooting?"

"That would be my best guess, but I haven't talked to Dex and it really depends on what his plans for the film are."

That makes sense. I guess I'll have to talk to Dex about it, I just feel like me going back to school is such a hassle, but I have a feeling he'll understand. How could he not?

"That should be fun, I guess," I say.

"You'll probably be sick of me by the time we get done filming and promoting the movie."

"I doubt that."

He flashes me a smile and I look down and as I start to blush. I pick at a loose thread on my pants and take a deep breath. If I didn't know any better, it would seem that our conversation turned playful... which is nice, since Spencer seemed upset just a few minutes ago, but I don't want to give him the wrong impression.

Spencer clears his throat after the most awkwardly

silent minute of my entire life. I was starting to think that it would never end.

"So… have you ever been to Colorado?" Spencer says.

"Nope."

"Oh."

"Why?"

"I was just curious… my mom lives there and there's a film festival, in Telluride… Dex mentioned he wanted to submit the film to it, but I have a feeling that we're far enough behind in production that it's not going to happen."

"That sucks."

"Yeah… I've been meaning to go visit her, but I just don't know that I'll get the time this year."

I look into his eyes and see that sparkle when he talks about his mom and it's obvious he actually has a good relationship with her. I used to think that's what I had. Things can just change so quickly. It's sad, really. I know that I'll never be able to have that kind of relationship with my mom… not after what she's done.

Spencer's phone rings and I hold my breath and he takes it out of his pocket and stares at the screen.

"Sorry… I've gotta take this."

I smile and nod at him as he swipes his finger across the screen and lifts the phone to his ear.

"Hey," Spencer says.

The look on his face shifts, he's looking a little irritated, as he stands up from the couch and walks toward the back door. Spencer opens the door and heads into the yard. Is it Monica that's calling him?

I take my phone out of my pocket and check to see if there's a text from Dex, even though I didn't feel my phone vibrate. There's nothing from him, so I decide to text Jess while I wait for Spencer.

Hey, I'm at Spencer's house… thanks for the help. I'm sure you're probably at work, but feel free to text me when you get home, I might still be up. I haven't heard from Dex, so I'll probably spend the night here.

I slide my phone back into my pocket since I don't expect to hear from Jess for at least a few hours.

Spencer walking across the yard draws my attention. He's still on the phone and he's looking really irritated. I feel a little bad... I'm sure the last thing he wants right now is to have me at his house. If there was any way for me to leave I would. It's another one of those times that I really wish I really had a car and could drive, for that matter.

With each moment I watch Spencer, I can see that he's becoming more and more irritated. I feel bad... he's so nice. It must have been Monica who called him. What else could have upset him this much?

I stand up from the couch and head out of the room. I noticed a door when I walked in that was slightly ajar, and I figure it's probably the bathroom. I open the door, it is a bathroom, and close the door as I flick on the lights.

I take a deep breath and lean against the door. I haven't really had time to sort out the emotions that are filling me. It was like I had to take off so quickly that I haven't even gotten to process the whole thing with my mom. I can't imagine having a kid and screwing up their life the way she has mine... it's just not right. She should have never had me if this is how she was going to be... and then we both would have been better off. I hate her so much.

Tears start to fill my eyes and I reach for the box of tissues sitting on the counter. I blow my nose, dry my tears and take a deep breath as I force myself to calm down. I can't trouble Spencer with anymore of my problems... not after how nice he's been to me.

"Amy!"

It's Spencer... he sounds a little panicked. I quickly toss the tissue in the trash and open the door. He's walking down the hall toward me and he looks relieved when he sees me.

"There you are... I was worried."

Why would he be worried about me?

"I… I just needed to use the restroom."

He smiles and nods.

"I… never mind."

"What?"

"Nothing… it's not a big deal. Sorry about that, the phone call… it was rude of me to answer a call and then leave the room."

We walk back into the living room and sit down on the couch. I sit in the same spot, but it seems like Spencer is sitting a little closer to me. I think.

"It's totally fine… I get it."

"Did you hear from Dex?"

I shake my head.

"Me either," he says.

Spencer shrugs and sets his phone down on the coffee table. Just looking at it, even from a distance, makes me sad that I broke the phone Dex gave me… I hate using this crappy phone.

Spencer looks back and tilts his head as he looks at me. I'm not sure what he's doing exactly, but it feels almost like he's studying me… it's kind of a little strange.

"Are you OK?" he says.

No, I'm really not, but I promised myself that I was done burdening Spencer with my stupid problems that must seem so insignificant to him.

"I'm fine, why?"

"Oh… it… I thought you looked like you had been crying."

"Nope… I'm good."

I swallow and force a genuine smile onto my face. Spencer smiles back and for at least that moment he seems convinced, which is unusual given his ability to read me like a book most of the time.

"Well, if you do need to talk about anything… you know I'm always here to listen."

"Thanks, you're sweet."

He's the guy that every girl wants… what they don't know is that he is really so much more than a pretty face. I guess maybe it's good for him that other girls don't know him the way I do because he would literally have to fight them off with a stick to leave his house.

"I'm serious… if you feel like you need to tell me something, Amy, don't hold back."

I want to tell him, I really do, because I have no one else to talk to right now, but I can't do it.

"Thank you."

Spencer turns his head and looks into the kitchen. I follow his gaze, but I'm not sure exactly what he's looking at.

"So," he says, "it's just after nine… do you want to have an early night or should we go do something?"

Spencer turns back to me with a smile on his face, but it's not the sweet smile… no, it's more devious.

"I… I don't know… it's been kind of a long day."

"Yeah… I just thought you might want to do something to take your mind off of everything… even if you don't want to talk to me about it, I can tell that something is bothering you."

The kindness in his eyes is begging me to give in. I don't really want to go out, I want to have an early night, but I have a feeling it might be the only way to distract Spencer from trying to find out what exactly is going on in the deep recesses of my mind.

"I guess that might be kind of fun… I don't want to be out super late though… tomorrow will probably be a long day."

Spencer smiles and jumps up from the couch.

"I promise we won't be out really late."

I grab my purse and follow Spencer through a door and into the garage. We get in his car and he starts it as the garage door opens behind us.

"Where are we going?" I say.

Spencer winks and flashes me a quick smile before

pulling his car out of the garage.

"It's a surprise."

He glances at me and starts to laugh. I guess the worried look on my face tells him everything he needs to know. I have no idea where he could possibly be taking me.

"Trust me, it'll be fun," he says.

I don't think I really have much of a choice…. The idea of trusting him has me a little worried, given my past with guys, but he's been nothing short of nice since I met him.

"I do… I trust you."

"I'm glad."

I turn my head and look at Spencer as he drives. He glances over at me and I expect to see a smirk on his face… but he looks completely serious. Is it possible that I've met someone who can be a true and good friend to me? I would like to believe that, but the fact that it's Spencer Thomas makes it more unbelievable, but so far since I've known him he's been amazing.

Neither of us says anything for the next few minutes as Spencer drives. I don't really recognize where we're going in the dark, but the houses quickly fade to businesses. There are people walking the streets, going in and out of the coffee shops and restaurants. It makes Greenville look like a ghost town and even though I would have been scared of a place like L.A. just a few weeks ago… I can't really explain it, but there's a part of me that's very excited about how lively it is here.

CHAPTER NINE

Spencer pulls the car into a parking lot and nods at the attendant. It's looks kind of sketchy... I don't know that I would park here if it was my car, but I guess he probably knows his way around here. Tall chain link fencing with razor wire surrounds the lot, which is shoehorned between two industrial looking buildings.

The lot is run down and I feel the cracks in the concrete as we drive over them. Some of the cars seem nice enough, nothing like Dex's, but some of them look like they were left here. Spencer pulls into a spot on the far end and we get out.

I glance over at Spencer, but he's looking at his phone as we walk. He looks up from his phone and gives a quick wave to the lot attendant. The man only responds with a slight nod of his head.

"He seems friendly," I say, once we are out of earshot.

Spencer laughs and turns toward me. I know it was kind of a mean thing to say, but I guess he thought it was funny.

"He actually is... I park there whenever I come here and he always keeps an eye on my car."

"Where is here?"

"We are in North Industrial," Spencer says.

Well… that explains all the scary looking buildings. I'm sure more than a few horror movies have been filmed in these buildings.

"And what are we doing here?"

"You'll see."

I guess it's possible that there's somewhere to go around here, why else would Spencer bring me here, but I have no idea what kind of place it could possibly be.

We turn a corner and I see it… it has to be the place we are going. A massive neon light, mounted above the door of one of the industrial buildings, is casting a glow on a crowd of people standing in line. There must be fifty or sixty people waiting to get in… this is going to take forever.

As we walk toward the back of the line, I see the door open and music pours out. It's loud… like really loud dance music, but it sounds good. The door closes and it fades just as quickly. The urge to dance has suddenly come over me and I just hope that it doesn't take forever to get in.

I walk up to the back of the line and stop. Spencer grabs my hand and pulls me to the side of the line. I flash him a confused face and he smiles back. Of course… why did I think we had to wait in line? I guess it's one of the many perks to being his friend.

A scary bouncer stands behind a rope at the front of the line, ready to stop anyone who tries to enter without his blessing, but when he sees Spencer he quickly steps to the side and lowers the rope.

"Thanks Craig," Spencer says.

"Good to see you, Sir."

I guess Spencer must come here all the time. A low murmur escapes the people waiting in line and I turn to see what's happening. It takes me a minute, but I finally realize that they are staring at us. I turn toward the door as it opens and Spencer pulls me inside.

"Who is she?" The last words I hear before the music assaults my ear drums.

It must have been one of the people at the front of the line. I don't know that I'll ever get used to having people stare at me everywhere I go because I'm with Spencer. It'll be nice to be just a normal person again once I head back to Salem.

Spencer turns around and I try to read his lips as he talks, but it's so loud that I feel like I can't even think. He leans in close to me… close enough that I can feel his warm breath against my neck. It sends a shiver through my body and it takes all of my mental energy to concentrate on what he says.

"Let's go to the VIP area and then we can dance."

I nod as he pulls his head away. We walk through a smallish entryway and into the main area of the club. To my surprise the music isn't actually any louder… I guess there must be speakers near the front door or something.

Spencer leads me through a crowd of people, but they don't seem to even notice him, to one of the back corners of the club. There's a section roped off and a guy standing in front of it with his arms crossed. He's wearing the same all black outfit and earpiece as the guy at the front door. He nods and steps aside, taking the rope with him, as he sees us walking up. I smile at him, but he doesn't respond at all.

The VIP area is nice, much nicer than the rest of the club. There are black couches along the back wall and glass coffee tables on the floor in front of them. Everything in the VIP area, and the whole club for that matter, is really modern looking and kind of reminds me of Dex's house. There's a bar on the left side of the area, but there isn't a bartender or anything.

Spencer finally lets go of my hand once we are in VIP. Normally I would have protested about him hanging on to me for that long, but I definitely have no desire to get separated from him in here. I'm sure I would be able to find him again, but I know it would cause a scene.

We sit down on one of the couches, the one in the very back corner and I let out a sigh. It feels good to relax… which is weird that I feel that way because it's so loud, but there's something calming about the whole scene. Although, I'm not sure exactly what the point of coming here is… it's not like we can have a conversation or anything.

I shake my head as Spencer tries to talk to me, but I can't hear a word. He smiles, nods and slides to the middle of the couch so that our shoulders are just inches from touching. My body feels warm, but I don't really know why… it's a little warm in here, but not hot enough to change my body like this.

Spencer leans his mouth close to my ear and moves my hair away from my face.

"Sorry it's so loud in here."

I nod and smile… it is loud, but it's not putting me off or anything.

"This is my favorite club to come to," he says.

I turn my head and yell into Spencer's ear.

"I've never been to… to a place like this before."

He has a surprised and amused look on his face when I pull back. I feel a little embarrassed and I don't know why… maybe it's because I'm such a small town girl and this is Spencer's life. I wonder how often he comes here? It must be a lot given how much the doormen seem to know him.

Spencer turns his attention to a young woman as she walks into the VIP area and comes over to us. I already don't like her as she flashes us a smile and leans over to say something to Spencer. He nods and she turns and walks toward the VIP bar area. I guess she works here, which would explain why she seems to know him. I'm not sure what it is about her that bothers me… but I feel Spencer put his hand on my arm and all thoughts about the pretty bartender vanish from my mind in the blink of an eye.

I turn my eyes toward him and he flashes me that million dollar smile and the girl fades from my mind as quickly as she appeared. I feel lost in his eyes when he holds up a glass… I guess I didn't even notice it appear. He holds it out to me… a glass with a clear liquid, mint, ice and black straw. I take the drink from Spencer and suck on the straw. The girl must have been a waitress or bartender. I look around for her as the sweet liquid flows through my lips and down my throat, but I don't see here anywhere.

It only takes a few minutes for me to finish my drink. I'm not sure what it was, but I feel much better now… relaxed and cooled down. It was sweet and minty, that's all I know. The waitress appears with another round just as I reach to set my empty glass down on the table.

She flashes me a smile and I force myself to smile back. There's something about her I still don't like, but I know I can't just go around not liking people for no reason… that makes me no better than any of these other people in L.A. and that's definitely not who I am or who I want to be.

Spencer leans toward me, putting his hand on my arm as he does so. His touch sends a wave of warmth through my body and I reach for my drink to cool me down.

"Do you want to dance?" he says.

I shake my head as I drain almost half the drink in one long sip. There's no way I'm going out on that dance floor with him… I wouldn't survive that. I set my drink down and lean toward him.

"You should… you go dance."

"Are you sure?"

I nod and flash him a smile. I don't want to stop him if he wants to dance. I'm perfectly happy just sitting here… not to mention, what would people think if they saw him out there dancing with me? He's good at just about everything, so I have a feeling that he's probably a great dancer and I would only make a fool of myself out there. I went to dances in high school, but this… this is an entirely different animal.

Spencer squeezes my arm, smiles and takes one last drink before jumping up from the couch and heading toward the dance floor.

I watch as he's swallowed by the crowd of beautiful people who move as one with the music. Part of me wishes I could be out there. I turn my attention back to my drink and try to nurse what's left of it as I flick my eyes back to the dance floor.

Every so often I see Spencer for a brief moment and I wish I was out there. I mean, I guess I could dance… maybe I'll have one more drink and by then I'll have worked up the courage needed.

I smile at the girl when she comes back with another drink and sets it down in front of me. As I drink it I start to feel something… I can't really explain it, but I feel relaxed and confident. I'm not sure why, but I'm liking it.

The next time I look toward the dance floor I see Spencer, but now he seems to be on the outskirts dancing with one specific woman instead of just dancing as part of the crowd. She puts her arm around his waist as she moves her head close to his ear. I'm not really sure… but… I feel jealous or something. I don't know why… it doesn't make sense, but for a brief moment I wish I was out there with Spencer, that I was the one whispering into his ear. I quickly push the thought from my mind. That's the last thing either one of us needs right now, not to mention I doubt that Spencer would ever feel that way about a small town girl like me. I have a feeling he sees me more as like a sister or a friend than anything else, which is totally fine and I would never expect our relationship to be anything other than that.

I take a deep breath as I finish my drink and set the very empty glass down. In my anxious attempt to decide what I should do, I was able to suck every last drop of liquid up through my straw, that and a piece of mint.

The dance floor is scary, but I want to be out there… I

want to be having the kind of fun that everyone else here is having. I feel like I need to stop letting myself be afraid of these kinds of experiences and now's a perfect time to start.

I stand up and pause for a moment. I feel a little light headed, which is weird, but it fades and I walk toward the dance floor. I don't see Spencer anymore, but that's fine... I wasn't planning on dancing with him or anything, but I wanted him to know that I didn't just disappear from the VIP area or anything like that.

The crowd swallows me as I let go and the music fills my body. It feels so natural as I give in and let my body move with each thump of the bass.

As I dance I feel like my whole world is spinning, but I'm not dizzy... no, I just feel amazing. I can't really explain it, but I feel like there's not a place I would rather be. Being on the dance floor just feels so right.

I smile as I feel a tap on my shoulder and turn around, expecting to see Spencer... instead standing in front of me is one of the most gorgeous men I have ever seen. I'm sure my jaw drops as I stare at him and try to soak him up. I blink to make sure that it's not a statue of a Greek god standing in front of me.

He flashes me a smile and I realize I've seen him before. Well, not in real life... I've seen him before, I think in a movie. He's not famous, not like Spencer at least, and I have no idea what his name is.

He puts his hand on my hip as we dance. Normally I would pull away, but I'm feeling amazing right now and I want to just go with the flow. We both move to the music and he slowly moves closer to me. I can feel the warmth from his body moving through his hand and into me.

I feel a tap on my shoulder and I turn around. Spencer is standing behind me and has a worried look on his face. He shakes his head a little and looks over my shoulder. I roll my eyes at him and turn back to my waiting dance partner. Spencer should know that I can look after myself just fine.

I flash the most adorable smile I can manage and go back to dancing. Any thought of Spencer vanishes from my mind in just a few seconds as the music works its way into my body. It feels so good to dance... this is making me wish I had done this before. I wonder what else I could have missed out on?

A hand grabs my shoulder, harder this time, and spins me around. I'm looking into Spencer's eyes and he looks scared, but I don't know why. He puts one hand around my waist and starts to lead me off the dance floor. I glance over my shoulder and see the disappointed face of my dance partner... I know I'll never see him again and it makes me kind of sad.

Spencer doesn't stop leading me away until we are back outside.

"What are you doing?" I say.

He shoots me an irritated glance and starts walking toward the car. I cross my arms and stand my ground... I'm not going to follow him until he tells me what's going on and explains why he just pulled me out of there.

"Let's go," he says.

Spencer doesn't stop and he doesn't turn around. I roll my eyes and wait for him to realize I'm not moving. It was rude... I was having a good time and dancing with a cute guy, which is exactly what I needed right now and he had to go and ruin it.

He finally stops, tilts his head back for a second and turns around. Spencer walks back toward me, glancing over my shoulder the whole time.

"Come on, I'll explain it to you in the car."

I shake my head. I want him to say it right now or I'm not going anywhere.

"Amy, don't do this... not right now."

He looks over my shoulder again, which is starting to get irritating and distracting. I turn and look to see what could possibly so interesting. Two paparazzi are standing next to the entrance of the club, one with a video camera resting on his shoulder and the other one has a camera with a massive zoom lens.

The paparazzi start walking toward us as I turn around and suddenly I feel scared. I'm not sure why, I know it's not rational, but for some reason they are making me feel uncomfortable. I wonder if this is how Spencer feels every time he sees them?

"Spencer, how are you?" the one with the video camera says.

Spencer takes my hand in his and pulls me down the sidewalk. I would have resisted, normally, but the presence of the paparazzi has made me feel really uncomfortable and now all I want to do is get out of here.

We hop in the car and Spencer is pulling away from the men just as I buckle my seatbelt. I look out the window and sigh as we drive by the club and I think about what could have been. I mean… it's not like I was going to marry the guy or anything, but it would have been nice to at least have a chance to talk to him and find out his name.

"What were you doing?" Spencer says.

"Me? What were you doing? You're the one who pulled me off the dance floor…."

I look over at Spencer just in time to see him flash me a dirty look before he turns his attention back to the road. Ugh. I'm so mad at him. I want to tell him how mean what he did was, but he's letting me sleep at his house and I don't want to risk that… I really have nowhere else to go.

"I don't get it," I say, "I was just dancing… the same as you."

Spencer sighs, but he doesn't say anything. I'm not sure he's acting irritated or upset… I'm the one who should be mad at him. I was starting to think that Spencer was different, not like the rest of the people in L.A., but now I'm not so sure.

"Do you have any idea who that was?"

There's a scary anger present in his voice and I can't tell

if it's directed at me or not. I close my eyes and take a deep breath to calm myself down. There's no sense in getting worked up over nothing, I know that.

"No," I say.

Spencer glances over at me and shakes his head.

"Who was he?"

"It doesn't really matter, but he's not a good guy and he has a certain… reputation when it comes to women…."

Spencer trails off and when I look over he's focused on driving. I sigh and just look out the window. I doubt there's anything I could say to him that would make any of this better because I can tell he's made up his mind about the guy a long time ago.

Ugh. My brain hurts. The more I try to think about the whole thing the foggier I feel. I close my eyes and lean back. I'm not sure why, but I'm feeling a little dizzy.

"I guess you're not a big drinker," Spencer says.

"What?"

It feels like needles stabbing my head as I open my eyes and turn my head toward him. I close them and this time slowly move my head. Was there alcohol in those drinks? Shit.

"How many drinks did you have?"

"Three… I think."

I had three, right? I'm starting to question even myself. It even hurts to think.

"Wow… that's… yikes."

Even his voice is starting to hurt my head. I guess Spencer is right, I have no tolerance for alcohol… which is why it would have been nice to know, I just sort of assumed there wouldn't be any since Spencer knows I'm underage.

I try to force myself not to think for the next few minutes… it just hurts my brain so much.

"I guess we need to get you some water and then put you to bed… I don't want you to be wrecked tomorrow, Dex would never forgive me."

I think about responding, but I know it would take more energy and effort than I'm willing to spare right now.

I do the only thing I feel like I can—I lean my head back and sigh. I hope we get back to his house soon... I just want to go to sleep and forget that any of this ever happened.

CHAPTER TEN

"Amy?"

I open my eyes as pain shoots through my head. I quickly look around and realize I'm still in Spencer's car before I can't take the pain anymore and close my eyes.

"Are you alright?" he says.

I nod my head just enough to let him know that I'm sort of alright. A bright light pierces my eyelids and I raise my hand to block it. I hear the driver's door close and the light fades. I reach for my seatbelt and take a deep breath as I try to ready myself to walk... a challenge I know I have to face and one that I'm certainly not ready for.

My door opens as I reach for the handle and I open my eyes. Spencer is smiling at me as he leans into the car, reaches around me and unbuckles my seatbelt. He moves his hand to my back and before I can even open my mouth he's lifting me out of the car.

Spencer puts me on my feet and closes the car door, but keeps his arm around my waist the whole time. I don't feel nearly as bad as I thought I would... and I definitely think I can walk into the house under my own power.

"Thanks," I say, "I'm... I'm good."

"You sure?"

I nod and Spencer hesitates for a few seconds, but finally lets go of me. He turns toward the door and I follow. I take two steps and then… then I lose my balance and start to fall.

"Ahhhh!" I yell.

I close my eyes and brace for impact, but it doesn't come. Instead, I feel Spencer's hands… they are under me as he cradles me and keeps me from falling. He slowly stands me up again, this time keeping his arm around my waist. Spencer takes my hand in his free one and walks me to the door. He lets go of my hand just long enough to open the door.

"Just take it slow," he says.

I nod as I focus on not falling again. It's not that I'm afraid… I know that Spencer will catch me if I do, but I'm embarrassed enough already and I think him saving me again would be too much… it would probably kill me.

We walk inside and Spencer helps me down a hallway, which I guess must lead to the bedrooms. He pushes open the first door on the right, while not letting go of me, and helps me inside. We make it to the bed, my world spinning the entire time, and he helps me sit on the edge of it.

Once he's convinced I'm stable, Spencer kneels on the floor in front of me and takes off my shoes. I close my eyes and take a deep breath as he stands up and puts his hands on my shoulders to steady me.

"Try to get some sleep… I'm going to go get you some water, you need to drink it before you fall asleep."

I nod as I lower my head to the pillow. I don't even bother climbing under the covers, I don't think I could manage if I wanted.

Spencer puts his hand on my shoulder and I open my eyes just enough to see him next to the bed with a glass of water in his hand. There's a straw in the glass and he holds it up to my lips. I take the straw in my mouth and start drinking. The cool water flows into my mouth and down my throat and for the first time I realize how thirsty I really

Emma Keene

was. I drink half of the glass before pulling my lips off the straw and moving my head back. Spencer turns and sets the glass on the nightstand.

"Please try to drink the rest before you fall asleep."

I have a feeling that's not going to happen… I feel so crappy that it's only going to be a matter of moments before I pass out.

Spencer brushes the hair out of my face and kneels next to the bed on the floor.

"Are you going to be OK?"

I nod, but only for a second because even the slight movement sends pain shooting through my head.

As I look into his eyes, I see it and I feel it… I think. That desire, deep inside of me, that I guess every other girl my age feels… the want to kiss Spencer. He's so close, close enough that I could move my mouth to his and press my lips against his lips. I know it would be amazing, how could it not be?

Obviously it's a terrible idea, but I feel like my body wants it enough that I can't stop myself.

I close my eyes and lean toward Spencer, expecting my lips to touch his at any moment. Instead, he pats me on the head and I open my eyes to see him standing up.

"Goodnight, Amy, get some sleep… and drink the rest of the water."

Spencer turns the lights off as he walks out of the room and the darkness surrounds me as he closes the door. I sigh as I reach for the glass of water and force myself to drink the rest of it. I put my head on the pillow and look up at the ceiling.

I suddenly feel very alone. I don't think it's the fact that I'm sleeping in a strange room… I'm sure it has something to do with my mom. I was so mad at her earlier, with reason, but if she leaves I might never see her again… which I'm OK with, I think, but that's it… if she leaves I have no parents left. Do I really want to live such a lonely life? I'm not sure I have much of a choice.

I roll onto my side and close my eyes. The pounding in my head isn't quite so bad now, but I'm starting to feel really tired, that and I feel like I can't keep thinking about everything that's happened in the last day or so... it's just making me sad.

Tomorrow will be better... it has to be.

CHAPTER ELEVEN

I open my eyes and look around the unfamiliar room as I try to figure out where I am. The night before comes flooding back to me as I sit up and the pounding in my head urges me to go back to sleep. I remember going to the club and coming back here, but I wonder if the part where I tried to kiss Spencer was real. I don't think I would let myself do something that stupid... would I?

I put on my shoes and stand up. I feel shaky, a little uneasy on my feet, but not nearly as bad as last night... well, from what I can remember of last night. I really hope that I didn't embarrass myself by doing anything stupid.

The clock on the nightstand says eight, later than I thought, which means we are probably late for filming... I hope that Dex isn't going to be mad at us. I head out of the room and toward the main part of the house. Spencer is standing at the sink with the water running. There is a faint aroma of food still hanging in the air, which must be from whatever he cooked himself for breakfast.

"Hey," I say.

He looks over his shoulder and turns off the water. Spencer smiles at me as he reaches for a dish towel and dries his hands. He sets the towel down and turns toward me.

"How did you sleep?"

"I... OK, I guess."

He lets out a little chuckle and shakes his head.

"How do you feel today?"

"Not great...."

Part of me wants to be upset with him, I feel mislead about last night... I didn't think he would offer me drinks with alcohol, but I also know that I should have asked or even just assumed since we were sitting in the VIP area of a club, which had a private bar. It's a mistake I regret and I won't make again, but I know there's really no point in even bringing it up with Spencer because I still have to see him every day, for now.

"That's unfortunate," he says. "So, sorry to change the subject... Dex called me a couple of hours ago, just to make sure you were alright and he wants you to call him."

I nod and feel for my phone, but it's not in my pocket. I guess it must be in my purse.

"On the dining room table," Spencer says.

I turn and see my purse sitting there. I walk over and take my phone out and see a missed call from Dex at just after six this morning. I pull up his number and walk over to the couch while it rings. I sit down just as he picks up.

"Hello?"

"Hey, Dex... it's me, Amy."

"Amy, how are you?"

I hesitate for a second, I'm not sure what Spencer told him and I would really rather not tell Dex about what happened last night.

"Fine... how are you?"

I do feel bad about not really being honest with him, but I need to remember that he's my boss. ·

"Good... so, I'm not sure how much Spencer told you...."

"Uh... he just said that you called to see how I was and that you wanted to talk to me."

There's a pause on the other end of the line and I can hear Dex clearing his throat.

"Well, your mom left... finally, this morning."

"Oh."

"Yeah... she said she's going back to Greenville, but I don't know for sure."

I wonder what she's planning... I have a feeling that she wouldn't just give up this life that easily. It's sad really, I share half my DNA with her and I hope that I don't end up like her.

"So," Dex says, "I... I don't know, but I feel like I need a couple of days off to decompress and figure some stuff out."

"Alright."

I'm not sure what that means, but he's the one paying for the movie and I'm not about to question his decision. I'm assuming he's referring to needing time to figure out what just happened, and maybe try to work things out with my mom, so I don't want to say anything that could get me into trouble if they get back together.

"I'm... leaving town... but Gina will be here, so you're more than welcome to just hang out and relax. I'm thinking maybe three or four days and then I'll be ready to get back to it. If it's going to be longer I'll give you and Spencer a call."

"Thanks, sounds good."

"And if you could just relay what I've told you to Spencer, it'll save me another call."

"Sure."

It's weird, he had a confidence in his voice before and now it's gone. I guess the whole thing with my mom really impacted him more than I realized. I feel kind of bad, it's not easy to be around her and I know part of why she got mad and left was because of me.

"Alright... and I'll have my phone if you need anything."

"OK."

I pull my phone away from my ear and end the call. Spencer is still in the kitchen, but walks toward me when he notices that I'm off the phone. He sits on the other end of the couch and smiles at me.

"So, what's happening with Dex?"

"He… he wants to take a few days off, like three or four, so he's shutting down the set for now and he's going out of town."

A look of surprise flashes across his face.

"Really?" he says.

I nod and look down at my phone. It's weird, it seems like neither of us were expecting that from Dex… especially since we both know that he's using his own money to make this movie. Hopefully, he'll be better in a couple of days.

"Yeah."

"Huh."

Spencer shrugs and stands up from the couch. He walks toward the back door and turns around as he reaches it.

"I'm going to make a quick call… I'll be right back."

I nod and turn toward the coffee table, where I noticed a magazine when I first sat down. It's a gossip rag, but it should be entertaining enough for the few minutes I expect Spencer to be on the phone. I start to flip through the magazine, not really seeing anything that looks all that interesting. The back door opens again and Spencer walks in, still on the phone.

"Alright… yeah… sounds good… love you, too."

Spencer smiles at me as he slips his phone into his pocket and walks over.

"So," he says, "how would you feel about a little trip?"

His question takes me completely by surprise… I definitely didn't expect him to say that.

"Uh…."

Spencer laughs and sits down on the other end of the couch. He looks into my eyes and I instantly want to say yes, I'll go with him, but I can't explain why.

"Sorry, I hope that didn't seem… forward, but I've been meaning to go visit my mom and since we have a couple day break I figured this would be a perfect time. I just thought that maybe you'd want to get away for a couple of days to put this whole thing behind you."

I know it's not going to be that easy, to forget everything that's happened in the last couple of days, but it's really sweet of Spencer to offer.

"I… I don't know what to say."

"Well, you can say that you'll go with me."

He flashes me his heartbreaking smile and winks at me. He's too much. I nod before I give his proposal a second thought.

Spencer dashes toward me, takes my hands in his and pulls me up. I smile as I land on my feet and he pulls me to the kitchen.

"Grab your purse," he says.

"Where are we going?"

He raises his eyebrow and starts to walk toward the door.

"To visit my mom."

"Right now?"

He nods and I follow him to the car.

"Don't you need to pack or something?" I say.

"Nah, I leave stuff at her house for when I visit."

Spencer pulls out his phone as he starts the car. I wonder what he's so focused on? He puts his phone in the cup holder and looks over at me.

"You ready?"

"I… sure, I guess," I say.

"Good."

Spencer smiles at me before turning his attention back to the car as he pulls out of the driveway.

"What about me? I need some clothes or something…."

"We don't have time… I'll just buy you some once we

get there."

I must have a surprised look on my face because Spencer starts to laugh.

"I can't let you do that," I say.

He doesn't respond, so I look over at him and I can tell that he's focused on navigating the traffic. It's still amazing to me how many people live here... I don't think I'll ever get over that.

"Sorry," he says, "I wasn't ignoring you... the only flight leaving LAX today with any seats left is in about an hour and with traffic we are already cutting it pretty close."

I smile at Spencer and turn to look out the window as he focuses on driving. I definitely didn't think this morning that I would be going anywhere other than to work, so this is kind of exciting... but at the same time I'm a little nervous about going to visit Spencer's mom.

Part of me is worried that his mom won't like me, which is stupid because we're just friends. I take a deep breath to calm myself down and I try to clear my head and focus on being in the moment. I was actually starting to feel a little worn down being around my mom, so at least that's done with and I'll get a chance to rest up the next couple of days and be in a much more positive mood once we start filming again.

"Your mom isn't going to mind me coming with you?"

"Of course not, she's looking forward to meeting you."

I'm not sure what to even think of that... how does his mom even know who I am?

"What do you mean?"

I look out my window as we drive by the LAX sign. I'm surprised it's so close to his house... it can't have taken us more than fifteen or twenty minutes.

Spencer looks over his right shoulder and changes lanes as he takes the exit for short term parking. I want to ask him again what he meant, but it can wait because he has a focused look on his face as he pulls into the lot and starts to look for a spot.

He parks the car and we get out. The whole place is full, the lights in the ceiling are struggling to make it even bright enough to see. It's a dingy and almost kind of scary place... not somewhere I'd like to spend more than a few minutes.

"You ready?"

"Yeah," I say, smiling at Spencer.

We're on a tight schedule and I feel my face turning red as I walk toward him. I don't want to be responsible for making us miss the only flight we can take.

Spencer smiles back at me and starts to walk. I walk quickly to catch up to him and we walk through two sets of sliding glass doors. As soon as we are inside things feel chaotic... there are people rushing in every direction and the noise is almost unbearable. The air is stagnant and hot, which is making it hard to breathe.

I follow him by a few long lines of people that end at counters staffed by airline personnel. Spencer turns and walks by a sign that says *First Class* and we walk up to the counter. The woman behind the counter is probably in her late forties, her brown hair is pulled back and she's smiling at us.

"Hello, Sir, are you checking in?"

"I actually need to book a ticket," Spencer says.

She wrinkles her brow as she looks us up and down, but it quickly fades... it's almost as she's trying to hide the fact that she was judging us.

"This is the line for first class, Sir... if you want to just go to the back of that line," she says, pointing at the seemingly endless line of people two counters down, "one of my associates will be more than happy to help you."

I turn to Spencer, who lets out a quick chuckle as he puts his hand in his back pocket and pulls out his wallet. He shakes his head, takes out a credit card and slaps it down on the counter. He seems a little irritated and I don't blame him... this woman was treating us like we couldn't fly first class, which I assume is because of our age.

"I want two *first class* tickets to Denver, on the eleven o'clock flight."

I can't help smiling at his emphasis on *first class*. The woman's eyes grow wide and she reaches for his credit card.

"And try to hurry, we don't want to miss the flight," he says.

She nods and turns her attention back to the computer. I lean against the counter and look around as I hear the clacking of a keyboard. There is a family in the other line, the parents and their daughter who looks about twelve or thirteen, and they keep looking over at us. The girl finally points at Spencer... I guess she must recognize him. I turn to Spencer, but he's not paying attention.

"If I could just have your ID, both of you."

I set my purse on the counter and fish through my wallet to find my ID card. I pass it to the woman, who takes it and stands it up against the top row of keys on her keyboard. She quickly pounds out my name on the worn keys and hands it back to me. Spencer hands over his driver's license and she does the same for him.

The woman sets a receipt on the counter and I catch a glimpse of it just after he signs it and before she takes it back. I blink a few times as I wonder if what I just saw was real. I think it said two thousand dollars and change... is that possible?

"If you could just set your bags on the scale," she says.

"We don't have any luggage," Spencer says.

"Uh... alright... well, I guess you can head to security then."

She sets two boarding passes on the counter and Spencer takes his and I take mine. I smile at the woman and she just stares at me. I can't decide if she looks irritated or confused or maybe some combination of the two.

"Have a nice day," I say.

She stammers, but I turn and walk after Spencer before

she can answer. People are so strange here. I wish she would have just been nice and done her job and it wouldn't have caused that weird tension between her and Spencer. I'm glad that's done with.

I step onto the escalator next to Spencer and he takes out his phone. I want to say something about flying first class, two thousand dollars is a lot of money, but I feel like it would be rude and that I shouldn't say anything… it's his money, after all, and he can do whatever he wants with it.

He puts his phone back in his pocket, turns to me and smiles.

"So, do you fly often?" he says.

I shake my head and look at my feet as my face starts to turn red.

"I… I've only flown once… my mom picked me up in Greenville and we flew on a jet that Dex got for us."

"Nice… gotta love the private jet. Sorry, but I'm not as much of a baller as Dex… so I hope you won't be disappointed in first class."

"I'm sure it'll be just fine."

I make a mental note to pay Spencer back for the flight once we finish the movie and Dex pays me. I know he probably won't take the money, but I want to at least offer.

"It's decent," he says, as we step off the escalator, "certainly much better than flying coach. Plus the flight isn't as long as from Greenville… it should only take a little over two hours."

I nod as we enter the security line. There's a decent amount of people in line, but it seems to be moving somewhat quickly. As we wind through the line and near the front, I notice people taking their shoes and belts off. I glance at Spencer, out of the corner of my eye, every few second until he starts to take his shoes off and I follow suit.

I follow his lead and put my purse and shoes in one of the gray plastic bins and slide it along the rollers that lead into what must be an X-ray machine. One of the security workers waves Spencer through a metal detector and holds her hand up, telling me to stop until he's clear of the area.

"Come through," she says.

I watch as she looks up at the machine as I walk through. Part of me is nervous that it's going to go off and I'll be in some kind of trouble. I don't think I have anything metal on me, but it's still in the back of my mind for some reason.

The woman nods at me and I walk to the end of the security area to collect my purse and shoes. I can't believe how crazy everything in this one little part of the airport is, but I guess it's good because it definitely makes me feel safer about flying.

I follow Spencer once we have our shoes back on. We walk by a newsstand that is brimming with activity… people seem to be stocking up on snacks and things to read for their flights. I'm enjoying watching the people here, they all seem to have so much purpose in their eyes as they ready themselves to fly.

"Here we are," Spencer says.

We walk toward a podium with a woman dressed in the same outfit as the weird lady at the first counter. We pass her our tickets and she quickly looks them over before ripping the boarding pass off and handing them back to us.

I follow Spencer down a long corridor that leads to the plane. It's weird… I can feel it moving as we walk, almost like it's swaying and flexing, but I'm sure they wouldn't have groups of people walking through it if it wasn't safe… it doesn't stop me from feeling a little uneasy though.

There is a flight attendant standing just inside the door of the plane. Spencer ducks as we step through and she smiles at us.

"Welcome aboard… do you need help finding your seat?"

"No, thanks," Spencer says.

She nods and I smile at her. Spencer turns to the right and I follow him to the second row of seats on the plane. I glance down the plane and see small seats, three on either side of the aisle. All the people smashed together remind me a little of sardines. I turn back to Spencer, who is in the window seat and putting on his seatbelt. I sit down on the leather chair and wiggle as I try to make myself comfortable. It's definitely not as comfy or roomy as the plane Dex got for me and mom, but it's a much nicer than what most of the people on the plane are experiencing right now.

The flight attendant walks over to us and smiles as she stands tall over us.

"Can I get you something to drink before we take off? Champagne or water... anything?"

The mere mention of Champagne reminds me of how much my head still hurts from last night. I shake my head and turn toward the window. I hear Spencer saying something to the flight attendant, but I'm watching another plane pull in next to us and I don't hear what they're talking about.

I close my eyes and sigh. I wish I were feeling better... I think I had adrenaline rushing through my body for the last hour as we got ready to come here, but now I'm starting to calm down and my headache is definitely more noticeable.

Maybe I'll try to sleep during the flight... I don't want Spencer to think I'm ignoring him or that I'm not grateful for this little trip. I turn to him and smile as the flight attendant hands him a bottle of water.

"Are you sure you don't want anything, Hun?" she says.

"I'm fine, thanks."

"Let me know if you need anything."

She flashes us one last smile before going to sit in her fold down seat near the front door of the plane.

"Are you alright?"

I turn to Spencer and nod. I wonder if he can tell that I feel like crap and that I'm a little nervous about flying. I'm sure everyone else on the plane thinks this is perfectly normal and they've been doing this for years, but for me... for me it's still an entirely new experience that I'm more nervous about than excited.

"It'll be over before you know it," he says.

I force a smile on my face and he smiles back before taking a long drink of water. He screws the cap back on his bottle and looks out the window. The plane rocks as we start to move backward and I grab the arm rests and squeeze them as tightly as possible. I close my eyes and force myself to keep breathing.

Calm down, Amy, you can do this... it's going to be fine.

CHAPTER TWELVE

"Here we are, Sir."

Spencer takes his wallet out and hands cash to the cab driver.

"Thank you," Spencer says.

The cabbie nods and smiles. I open my door, get out and Spencer slides across the back seat and follows. He closes the door and I wait for him to start up the walkway to his mom's house.

It's a nice house, nothing like Spencer's... but compared to the rest of the houses in the neighborhood it's seems refined. There are two pillars, one on either side of the red front door. Windows line both the floors of the white house. It has a certain charm that reminds me of what I would expect to see in the typical American neighborhood... I like it.

Spencer presses the doorbell and I hear it chime on the other side of the door. He told me once during the flight, and twice during the cab ride, to relax and that coming here was fine, but I still feel nervous about meeting his mom and I'm not sure why. When I think about it logically he's right, we are just friends, but for some reason I feel like a girlfriend that is being taken to meet her boyfriend's parents for the first time… and I'm nervous.

The door opens and his mom is standing in front of us with a big warm smile and I instantly feel relieved, my stress evaporates before she even opens her mouth.

"Hiiiiii!"

I can see where he gets his infectious smile from. She steps forward, wraps her arms around me and pulls me close. I put my arms around her and hug back. It's nice, a warm feeling passes through me that I hadn't felt in a long time… the warm embrace of a truly loving parent.

She pulls back, puts her hands on my shoulders and stands back as she looks me up and down.

"It's nice to meet you, Mrs. Thomas," I say.

She smiles, lets go of me and waves my comment off.

"Please, call me Brenda… and it's very nice to meet you, too, Amy."

"Hi, Mom."

Spencer puts his arms around his mother and they share a brief hug that ends with her kissing him on the cheek.

"Come on in," she says.

Brenda steps aside and we go inside. She follows and closes the door behind us. The house is nice inside, again, not decorated the way a house in L.A. would be, but more in sort of a middle of the country way that works perfectly with the exterior… it's cute.

"You have a beautiful home, Mrs. Th… Brenda."

"Where did you find her, Spencer?"

I let out a nervous laugh as I start to blush. The playful tone in her voice makes me think that Spencer hasn't really explained to her who I am and that she might be thinking I'm his girlfriend or something.

She smiles at me again, turns and walks down the hall. I look to Spencer and he nods in her direction, so I follow her. I can hear Spencer walking behind me as his sneakers squeak with each step he takes on the wood floor.

"I made some sandwiches," she says. "I hope you guys

are hungry."

I'm definitely starting to feel hungry, finally, after not really eating today. We walk into the kitchen and there is a plate of stacked sandwich halves that have been cut into perfectly equal triangles.

Spencer grabs a sandwich, puts it on one of the plates sitting on the counter and hands it to me. I smile and lift the sandwich to my mouth. Peanut butter and blueberry jelly. It's so good that I'm already on my second bite before Spencer has his own.

"So, Spencer, how's the movie going?"

He finishes chewing and sets his plate back on the counter.

"Do you want to sit down?" Brenda says, looking at me.

"I… I'm fine… we were sitting for the last three hours."

She smiles and nods before turning her attention back to her son.

Spencer answers his mom, but by that time I've got another bite of sandwich in my mouth and I'm not paying attention to them. Well, I'm looking at Spencer and Brenda, it's just my thoughts that are miles away.

Without a second consideration I start thinking about how many other girls Spencer has brought home to meet his mom… I wonder if it's been a lot. She seemed excited to meet me, which I guess she could have just been acting that way to make Spencer happy… but I really doubt that, I didn't get a weird feeling from her at all. I quickly push the silly thought out of my head. I'm still upset about Logan, even though I buried those feelings deep down, so I don't know why I would think about Spencer like that. Not to mention I know he would never be interested in a girl like me.

"Amy?"

I nod and realize that Spencer and Brenda are both looking at me like I'm supposed to answer a question.

"Sorry," I say, "I was... I got distracted."

Brenda laughs and puts her hand on my arm.

"It's fine, dear, I'm sure you're tired from the flight. Do you two want to take a nap before dinner?"

It's funny to think about dinner... I just quickly polished off a whole sandwich, but a nap... a nap sounds amazing. I'm still not feeling great from last night and I know the only thing that's going to fix that is sleep.

I turn to Spencer just as he covers his mouth and yawns. I guess I'm not the only one who is thinking about sleep.

"I guess that might be a good idea," he says.

Brenda smiles and turns to me.

"If you want to follow me, I'll show you to your room."

I nod and walk out of the kitchen after her and back to the entry way. We head upstairs and turn right when we get to the top. She walks by an open door and extends her arm. I walk in and she follows me. It's decorated like the rest of the house, but it has a distinctively feminine touch to it, especially with light pink walls. I wonder if it was a girl's bedroom at some point, but Spencer never mentioned anything about having a sister.

"The bathroom is just across the hall, Spencer's room is the one next to yours and mine is at the other end of the hall."

"Thank you, so much, really... it's so nice of you to let me stay here."

She smiles and wraps her arms around me again. I already like her... she seems just so nice and lovely to be around. I might just have to scold Spencer for not visiting her enough because if my mom was like Brenda my life would have been so much easier.

"No problem... I'm glad Spencer came to see me, even for a short visit, and I'm glad that he brought you with him. It's nice to have another girl in the house."

She smiles at me, but it's like something is wrong... it's

like a deep sadness has filled her eyes. Brenda nods, turns and walks out of the room. I wonder what could have possibly could have made her look that sad.

I close the door, set my purse down on the dresser and take my phone out before sitting on the bed. I lay back and look at the ceiling as I wait for my phone to turn on… I guess I forgot to do it after we landed.

I don't have any messages, so I decide to text Jess since I haven't heard from her since yesterday. I feel like she's the only person in my life I can actually talk to and I really haven't even known her for that long… it's weird to not have anyone left from my life in Greenville. I guess my closest tie to my hometown is Dex, which is weird.

Hey, I meant to text you earlier, but today has been a little crazy…. hope you're having a good day. Miss you.

I set my phone down on my chest and close my eyes while I wait to see if she'll respond before I drift into sleep. I meant to ask Brenda when I should get up, but this bed is so comfy… there's no way I'm going to get up now. I'm sure they will just come and get me whenever.

My phone vibrates.

Hey! I miss you! What's going on? Did something happen with Spencer last night? Were you a bad girl?

I can't help but laugh. Jess always sends me the most ridiculous texts and I love the fact that she's questioning whether or not I did something bad last night, especially when she knows that I didn't, but I'm sure she wishes that I was bad a little more often… I feel like she gleans some satisfaction out of it and not in a weird way, but in a she wants me to have fun kind of way.

No, I wasn't bad. Well, I mean we went to a club and I had a couple of drinks, on accident, but that was kind of it.

On accident? How does that happen? I hope you at least made out with Spencer or something.

It hits me while I'm thinking about how to reply… I remember something from last night, something I didn't think I would and maybe in part because I didn't want to remember it. Did I really try to kiss Spencer? Ugh... I'm such an idiot. I'm sure he had a good laugh over that. He probably brought me here because he felt bad for me.

I sigh and type a response to Jess before she thinks I forgot about her.

No, I didn't make out with Spencer. I accidently had a couple of drinks because I didn't realize they had alcohol... I'm kind of dumb like that.

I shake my head. I do feel a little bad about skirting around the truth, with Jess. It's true that I didn't kiss Spencer, but I'm not about to admit to her that I tried and failed. It's too much, I think I would rather die than admit that.

I'm sure Spencer won't forget about it anytime soon... I just hope that he never brings it up because I have no excuse for how I acted. Hopefully he's not mad at me or anything.

Boooo. You're literally no fun at all.

I laugh and shake my head at her text. I hope that we can be friends for a very long time and she never changes because I love who she is.

I know, sorry to disappoint you. Maybe you can show me how to get in trouble once I get back to Salem.

I'm actually really looking forward to hanging out with her again. School is going to be whatever... I know it's important to get my degree, but I feel like I'm grasping at straws to have some kind of meaningful friendships so I really can't wait to see her.

You know I will. So are you back at Dex's house now?

I smile as I read her text. I know she will and I'm actually kind of looking forward to it. I'm not excited to get in trouble, but the idea is kind of fun.

No... I'm actually in Colorado now. It's kind of a funny story, but basically Dex wanted a couple of days off, so he let us have some time off. Spencer said he's been meaning to visit his mom and he didn't want me to be alone at Dex's, so we flew here and just got in a little while ago.

I put my phone back on my chest and close my eyes. Jess should get a kick out of that. I'm sure she's going to think there's something going on between us now.

My phone vibrates just as I feel myself drifting off into sleep and I can't bring myself to get it.

CHAPTER THIRTEEN

"Amy?"

I blink three times and lift my head. Brenda is standing in the doorway of the room and it takes me a second to realize where I am. I smile back at her as I sit up in bed and swing my feet over the side.

"Yeah?"

"It's time for dinner, if you want to come on down."

I nod and move my hand over my mouth as I yawn. She smiles, turns and walks down the hall. I grab my phone to check the time… it's just after five. Wow, I can't believe I slept for that long, I was expecting a quick nap. My head doesn't hurt anymore, though, so I guess I needed it more than I realized.

There's a message from Jess, on my phone, which I read while walking down the hall and the stairs.

Omg! That's crazy! I knew there was something going on between you and Spencer… nothing you say can change my mind, not now. You sly little fox, you.

I shake my head and put my phone into my pocket. I'll text her back later, before bed. I have a feeling she's right… I probably won't be able to change her mind, but I'm definitely going to try because the last thing I need is her blabbing to people in Salem that I'm dating Spencer Thomas. I guess there's the distinct possibility that Logan already did that, though. Such is life.

Spencer is already in the kitchen when I get downstairs and he's helping his mom cook. He turns around when I walk in and flashes me a smile. He's wearing an apron, too, which says *Kiss the Cook*... it's rather appropriate given last night. Ugh... is he really going to give me a hard time about it?

"Hey," he says, "how was your nap?"

"Good... I feel much better, now, thanks."

He points at one of the chairs at the small table against the back wall of the kitchen. It really looks more like a breakfast table, it's a little on the small side, but there are three places already set.

"Can I do anything?" I say.

"Sit down, dear, please... dinner is almost ready."

"Are you sure?"

She nods and waves a wooden spoon in my general direction. I pull out the chair on the end and Spencer stops me.

"No, Amy... the middle one is you."

I raise my eyebrow and look at him, but he's already back to cooking. I sit down and look around the room. It's kind of weird... there are some family photos on the wall, but they are just of Spencer and Brenda. There's a dog in a couple of them, a golden lab, but no man. Spencer never has told me anything about his dad. I'm a little curious, but I'm definitely not going to ask... not while we're here at least, maybe when we get back to L.A., maybe.

Brenda opens the oven and the smell of herbs wafts through the room. It instantly makes me hungry and I feel my mouth starting to water. I wonder what they are making. If Spencer's cooking is any indication of what his mom cooks like, I have a feeling I'm in for a treat.

"So... are you going to see any of your friends while you're here?"

"No, I don't think so. We won't be here that long and I kind of just want to relax," Spencer says.

"He still has friends here, but doesn't really stay in contact with them. Most of them are getting married and starting families," Brenda says, turning and looking at me.

"That's nice," I say.

I'm not sure how else to even respond to that.

"Do you go visit your friends in Greenville?"

I raise my eyebrow. I'm surprised that she knows where I'm from and that she didn't ask about my parents. I guess Spencer must have told her more about me than I expected.

"Uh, no, not really… I don't have any friends left there and it really hasn't been that long since I was there."

"Mom."

"Sorry," she says. "Spencer gets irritated that I ask so many questions."

"It's fine, really," I say.

"See," she says, "she doesn't mind, Spencer."

"Don't feel obligated to answer," Spencer says.

She smacks his arm and he smiles at me.

"Amy, how's the movie going?"

"Good… fine, I guess. I don't really know. I've never done this before, so I have no idea if I'm doing a good job or if I'm awful."

"I'm sure you're brilliant."

"I doubt brilliant… maybe adequate, but if I'm awful, I don't think Dex or Spencer would have the heart to tell me."

Brenda waves a wooden spoon at me and shakes her head.

"You're not adequate. Spencer has told me several times that he's impressed with how quickly you picked things up."

Huh. I guess Spencer told his mom about me on more than one occasion. It's a little strange, but I blow it off because it probably means nothing. I'm sure they talk often enough that they run short of conversation and maybe Spencer mentioned me a couple of times.

"Ma."

"Sorry... sorry."

She's funny and it's cute to see her get under his skin a little. I can see where he picked up that ability. He's always teasing me and thinks that it's funny, but now... now the tables are turned and he gets to see what it's like.

Spencer looks over at me and just shakes his head, but he's smiling. I have a feeling he's thinking the same thing I just was. It's funny though... I sometimes found it irritating, but now that I see where he gets it, well, I find it a little endearing and cute.

"Well," Brenda says, "that should do it."

Spencer carries a large wooden bowl of salad to the table and Brenda brings a whole chicken that she's just finished carving. I feel like I'm leaning over the chicken to absorb the wonderful aroma.

"It smells amazing," I say. "I feel so lame for sleeping and not helping with dinner."

They sit down, Spencer on my left and Brenda on right, and she puts her hand on my shoulder.

"You're our guest... please don't feel like you need to do anything."

"Thank you."

"Amy actually helped me with dinner last night."

Spencer serves me some salad and then passes it to his mom. She starts with chicken and then slides the plate toward me. I serve myself a few slices of breast and pass it to Spencer. The salad looks as good as the chicken smells.

"Do you cook a lot?" Brenda says.

"Uh... no, I pretty much don't cook at all. My mom, she was a teacher... so she was home early enough to cook dinner every night and she always said teaching me was more trouble than doing it herself."

A frown briefly crosses her face as she chews a bite of chicken.

"She's a quick learner, though," Spencer said.

"Hopefully you get more chances to cook with Spencer," she says, winking at me.

I blush as I realize what she's saying and look down at my food. I spear some chicken and lift my fork to my mouth. It's perfect... really moist and tender.

"The chicken is really good," I say.

"Thank you," Brenda says, "the rosemary adds a nice touch, I think."

"It's good, Mom."

She smiles at him and I take a bite of the salad. It's equally good. The lettuce is crisp and the flavors meld together perfectly. From what I can tell there's carrot, celery, egg and some cheese in it. I eat another bite of salad and switch back to the chicken.

"Thank you," she says, flashing me a smile.

I'm glad I came to visit. When Spencer first suggested it I wasn't interested, but I was basing that on my relationship with my own mom. Brenda is so nice though. I would be more than happy to live with or visit my mom all the time if she were like Brenda. It does make me sad... I wish I could have that kind of relationship with my mom, but I know that it'll never happen.

"What are you two working on next? Any films lined up?"

"I've got a couple of scripts that I've been looking at," Spencer says. "They're the usual stuff, though. I guess I should be happy that I got to do this film with Dex, it was a really nice change."

"And what about you, Amy?"

I shake my head and finish chewing before I answer Brenda.

"I'm going to school."

"Yeah?"

I shrug as I stab a piece of chicken with my fork.

"Yeah... this acting thing was just a chance happening. I was always planning on going to college. I'm glad though, it gave me a chance to make some money so that I don't have to wait tables again anytime soon."

I lift the chicken to my mouth and look at Brenda. She sets her fork down and takes a drink of water before looking at me.

"Don't forget, Dear, sometimes a rare opportunity is given to us and we need to be able to recognize that."

"Yeah."

I get what she's saying, but she hasn't seen me act. I know there's no future in it for me, but it's sweet of her to have faith in me considering we've just met.

CHAPTER FOURTEEN

Brenda wraps her arms around me and squeezes me so I tightly I feel like I might pop.

"I wish you could stay longer," she says.

"Me too, mom," Spencer says.

She finally lets me go and I feel the air returning to my lungs. I'm so glad that Spencer invited me to come with him to visit her... she's a sweet woman and the kind of mom I wish I had. He's a lucky guy and she's a lucky woman to have such a good man for a son.

"Thank you so much for having me."

She smiles at me, takes my hands in hers and looks into my eyes.

"You are very welcome, dear. Please come visit again and maybe you can get my son to come visit me more often."

I'm not even sure how to respond to that... it sounded like she was implying that we're dating. I wonder what Spencer told her about me? I just smile and nod, it's the only thing I can think to do.

"And you," she says, turning to Spencer, "you better bring her back next time... she's a sweet girl and you had better be good to her."

"I… uh, mom…."

"Spencer, just treat her right and she will be good to you. I can see in her eyes how much she cares for you… don't ever take that for granted."

My eyes grow wide with each passing word. I look to Spencer, who just shakes his head, smiles and kisses his mom on the cheek.

"Sure thing, mom."

He wraps his arms around her and gives her a long hug. I get why he's not trying to argue with her, but he's going to have to explain our relationship to her at some point… standing on her front step with a taxi waiting for us and flight to catch isn't exactly the right time.

Spencer lets go of his mom and I see a tear forming in the corner of her eye as we turn and head for our taxi. She loves him and wishes she could see more of him, that much is clear, but it's also obvious she understands that he has his own life and that he does his best to visit him when he can. It's a relationship that I envy, it's one I can never have with my mom.

I get in the taxi first and slide across the seat. Spencer gets in and closes the door.

"To the airport, please," he says.

"Yes, Sir."

Spencer waves out the window to his mom. She waves back before heading inside as the taxi pulls away from the house.

I have a feeling that I'll never see her again, which is kind of sad… I really like her, but I know that there will never be a reason for me to come back here. I'm sure Spencer will have a new girlfriend soon and will take her to meet his mom the next time he visits. I feel a twinge of jealousy… I just hope that whoever she is, she realizes how awesome Brenda is.

"Sorry about that," Spencer says.

"About what?"

"I… I'm not sure if you notice, but I think my mom is

under the impression that we're dating."

"Yeah, I noticed."

"I wanted to tell her, but she loved you and I couldn't find the right moment or the right words to tell her that we are just friends."

I feel a sharp pain in my chest. I know it's the truth... I've known that all along, but hearing it from Spencer makes it hurt just that much more.

"That makes sense."

I suddenly feel sick and roll down my window to get some fresh air.

"Are you alright?"

"Fine... I... I just wanted some air, I'm warm."

I see Spencer take out his phone and I look out the window as the car pulls onto the highway. I can't believe the trip is over already, but I'm ready to get back to filming... the sooner we get back to that the sooner we can be done and I can go back to Salem.

When Dex called this morning and said he was ready to start filming again tomorrow he sounded different... calm really, like he had done whatever he needed to do. I wonder if he went to go see my mom in Greenville. I wanted to ask, more out of curiosity, but I decided that he would have or will tell me if he feels like it.

"Thanks for coming with me," Spencer says.

I nod as I watch the world whiz by. It's rude to not answer Spencer, I feel kind of bad, but I feel like I'm in such a weird space right now. The whole thing with my mom is still only a few days old and very fresh in my mind and now... now Spencer's mom thinking we are a couple makes me uneasy for some reason.

Neither one of us says anything until we close in on the white peaks of the Denver airport. I can feel the tension in the car and the driver constantly looking in his rearview mirror isn't making it any easier.

"Sorry to bother you, Sir," the driver says, "but are you Spencer Thompson? The actor?"

"Thomas."

"Sorry?"

"Spencer Thomas," Spencer says, an obvious edge in his voice.

"Yeah, Spencer Thompson… is that you?"

Spencer sighs, clearly aware that the driver isn't going to get it.

"Yes."

"Would you mind signing an autograph for my daughter? She's a huge fan of yours… even has a giant poster of you on her wall."

"Sure, when we stop."

The driver smiles and nods as he turns into the departure area of the airport. He pulls the car up to the curb and puts it into park. He hands Spencer a pad of white paper and a black pen.

"What's her name?"

"Sarah."

Spencer writes *To Sarah, Best Wishes… Spencer Thomas* and hands the paper and pen back over the seat.

"Thank you, so much, Sir… I really appreciate it."

I open the door and climb out of the car while Spencer pays for the cab ride. The same stiff wind is blowing as when we got here, making it chillier than I would have expected for this time of year. I look at the mountains, looming large, and I guess I shouldn't be surprised by the air temperature—there's still snow on the highest peaks and it's summer. Crazy. I can't even imagine what living here in the winter would be like.

Spencer gets out of the cab and closes the door. He looks at me and brushes his hair off his forehead. He's upset, that much is obvious, but I'm not sure why. Could it be just because the guy messed up his name? I really doubt it, especially since he still signed an autograph for the guy's daughter.

"What's wrong?" I say.

He blinks and looks into my eyes. It's not the same soft

look that he usually has... no, there's pain there, the same pain that I saw in his mom's eyes when we first got to her house.

"Can I tell you something?"

I feel my heart beating faster. I'm afraid of what he's going to say, but I can tell by the look on his face that he needs to tell me.

"Sure."

"My mom... the reason why I didn't say anything to her about us... well, it's because she... she... I haven't seen my mom this happy in a really long time. It's been years, Amy, since she was like this."

Spencer tilts his head back and I can see his chest heave as he takes a deep breath of the crisp Colorado air. He looks back at me and I would swear that he looks like he's about to cry.

"I can't stand to see her so sad... I just... I can't do it. When she met you, she... she just lit up."

"What happened?"

"My...."

Spencer closes his eyes and shakes his head. I can tell it's not going to be easy for him to say. Whatever it is that was so painful for his mom was just as hard for him. He opens his eyes and forces a smile onto his face.

"We are going to miss our flight."

He turns and starts walking toward the terminal. I open my mouth, but before I can utter a single word he is already out of earshot with this much wind. I hurry after him and manage to catch him as the double glass doors slide open.

I put my hand on Spencer's shoulder, but he doesn't stop walking.

"You can tell me, whatever it is," I say.

"It's fine... I'll tell my mom the truth. She'll understand."

I wrinkle my brow. I wonder what could have made him change his mind about telling me... and telling his mom the truth. I feel kind of bad, she did seem really happy, but that's his choice to tell her, I never said anything about it to him.

We walk to the first class check in counter. Spencer has his wallet out and credit card on the counter before the woman even says anything.

"We need two tickets to LAX on the next flight," he says.

"Sure thing, Sir... if I could just see your ID."

Spencer hands over his driver's license and I give her my ID. She looks at his and smiles at him. It's obvious that she recognizes him, but she doesn't say anything... which is actually kind of surprising. Maybe she can tell by the look on his face that he's not in the mood.

The woman behind the counter types our information into her computer and hands back my ID and his license. She flashes him a smile and goes back to getting our tickets.

"Spencer, please... you can talk to me. You listened to me whenever I needed to talk about anything. I want to do the same for you."

His body goes rigid, so I know he heard me, but he doesn't answer me or even turn to look at me. Ugh. This is going to be a long flight back. All I can really do is give him space and hope that eventually he will tell me what happened, I just want to help... I wish he could see that.

CHAPTER FIFTEEN

I look out the window as the ground approaches at a speed I'm still having a hard time grasping. It's amazing how quick, and scary at the same time, the whole traveling by plane thing is.

The flight was about how I expected—Spencer was quiet the entire time, mostly pretending to be asleep as a way of avoiding conversation. I slept a little, but mostly just flipped through the in-flight magazine and watched a little bit of TV. Hopefully the car ride isn't quite so boring.

"Welcome to Los Angeles, Ladies and Gentlemen," the pilot says, through the intercom. "We thank you for choosing us for your travel needs. If there's anything else we can do for you, please let one of the flight attendants know or proceed to the customer service counter. Once again, thank you, we appreciate your business and we hope to see you soon."

The intercom crackles as he finishes. I glance at the first class attendant, she seemed nice, but she looks irritated and a little tired... I don't think she notices me looking at her. It must be a hard job, I can't even really fathom the long hours and endless travel.

We get off the plane as we reach the gate and I have to

hustle to keep up with Spencer. He doesn't even look at me until we are outside.

"I… I think it would be best if you just took a cab."

I look into his eyes and he quickly turns away. He's not mad at me, at least I don't think he is, but that deep sadness is still in his eyes. I was hoping that it would have faded during the flight. I nod and walk toward the curb where there are a few taxis waiting. Hopefully, if I give him space he will change his mind… I really want to be there to help him with whatever it is that he's going through.

Spencer opens the door of the cab for me and I get in. Before I can say anything to the driver, Spencer sticks his head through the open passenger window and hands the guy a wad of cash.

I take out my phone and turn it on as Spencer tells the driver Dex's address. I look at him and force myself to smile, even though looking at him makes me sad and he just looks at me with a stone face.

"I'll see you tomorrow," he says.

He steps away from the curb and walks off as the taxi pulls away. I look forward and see the driver looking in the rearview mirror.

"Was that… Spencer Thomas?" he says.

"Wow… that's cool, how do you know him?"

I sigh and take a deep breath. I'm really not in the mood to discuss my personal life with a random taxi driver.

"He's a friend."

I look down at my phone and hope that he doesn't bother me anymore. Normally I wouldn't mind—nice people seem pretty few and far between in this town, and he seems alright, but I feel so out of sorts from Spencer. I know it's not his fault, but I'm just so used to him being in such a great mood all the time… it's so weird to see him like this.

There's a text from Jess waiting for me and I realize that I never texted her back after my first night in

Colorado. I feel bad and decide to text her back right away. I'm sure she probably thinks I fell off the planet or that I've been busy doing things she would approve of with Spencer.

Amy, I never heard back from you. I'm going to go ahead and assume that you've been 'busy' with Spencer. Hope you're having fun, text me back when you get back to L.A. or wherever. No rush. Love you.

I can't help but smile as I read her text. It's amazing, but so far having her as a friend since my first few days in Salem has really been the only constant in my life. I have no idea what I would do without her.

You wish. I just got busy. Just landed in L.A., heading back to Dex's house right now.

I look out of the window as the car slows. It's near the middle of the afternoon and we are hitting traffic… I think… either that or this is normal. I'm not really sure, but there are cars everywhere.

My phone vibrates in my hands and I look down to read the reply from Jess.

Yay! I missed you. How was your trip? Did you have fun? What about Spencer's mom? Was she nice?

So many questions.

It was pretty good… it was nice to go somewhere and not have to worry about my mom and her drama for a couple of days. His mom is amazing… she was really nice and seemed to be actually interested in what I thought about things, which is quite the change from talking to my mom.

I hit send and look up. I didn't even notice, but we are on the street where Dex lives and the driver is slowing down to try and find the house.

"Who lives here?" he says, as he pulls up in front of the gate.

"Thanks."

I get out of the car without answering his question. I know Gina mentioned to me before that Dex wasn't exactly keen on people knowing where he lived and the last person I wanted to tell was a taxi driver… he could potentially tell a lot of people.

The gate swings open as I walk up… I guess Dex or Gina must have noticed the car pull up outside. I walk up to the front door and it opens just as I lift my hand to knock. Dex is standing in front of me with a goofy smile on his face.

"It's good to see you," he says.

"You too."

He steps forward and hugs me… something I wasn't expecting, but I'm certainly glad he's back in a good mood. I guess he worked out whatever was going on. Part of me really hopes that he didn't make amends with my mom. I know it's possible, but I think he would have told me on the phone if that was the case.

"Come in, I've got a couple things I need to talk to you about."

That sounds a little ominous….

Dex laughs and steps away from the door to let me in.

"Don't look so worried," he says, "it's nothing major… certainly nothing that would warrant that kind of panicked look on your face."

Once again, I've embarrassed myself by being completely emotionally transparent. Wonderful. I really need to work on that. I remember when I was growing up, my dad would tell me to stay calm and keep my emotions in check. I guess he didn't realize who he was talking to.

"Sorry," I say.

I force myself to look more normal as I follow Dex through the house and onto the back porch. It's a little warm out, especially after spending the last few days in Colorado, but Dex doesn't seem fazed by it. We walk down to the pool and sit in chairs next to it. It's looking really refreshing right now… I wish I could dive in. Maybe I'll go for a swim later.

"So," Dex says, "are you ready to get back to work? I want to finish up in the next couple of weeks… I know it's a lot, but I think if we push hard we can get it done. I want you to be able to go back to school in time for the start of it."

My eyes grow wide and Dex smiles in response.

"Is… is that possible?"

"I think so. We're just going to change up the shoot a little and just do all of your scenes first. If for some reason something doesn't come out… well, I was thinking that maybe if we needed to reshoot something you'd be amenable to flying out on a weekend."

It's not at all what I expected to hear from Dex. I somehow expected that he was going to tell me some bad news or something, like maybe it was going to take even longer than he originally thought.

A hundred thoughts fly through my brain. I had already mentally prepared myself to miss the beginning of school… I guess I'm going to have to get registered for classes in the next few days and then….

I realize there's really no point in getting myself worked up, not yet at least. Dex said he hoped that it would be possible and he sounded fairly sure, but I'm really trying to not get my hopes up. I would hate for the shoot to run long, after I got ready to go back to Salem in time for school, and then not be able to.

"That's great… and yes, of course I could fly out on a weekend. Whatever you need, Dex."

He smiles at me sits back in his chair. It's kind of amazing, he looks more relaxed in this moment than I've ever seen him. I open my mouth to ask about my mom, but I stop myself… I know it's a bad idea and it would probably just upset him. Another time, maybe, when he's ready to talk about it.

"Good."

Dex spreads his lips and leans forward, as if preparing to say something else, and then sits back and shifts his gaze to the pool.

"What is it?" I say.

"Oh… I meant to bring it up before, but I wanted to make sure that you and Spencer had a chance to build some on-screen chemistry first… tomorrow's scene has a kiss. It's a fairly lengthy one, too, but I wanted you to know about it so you didn't feel blindsided by it on set."

I shift my eyes from Dex to the pool and stare into the calm water. I'm not even sure what to think. It's weird… I tried to kiss Spencer a few days ago and he made sure that didn't happen and now… now we have to kiss. I wonder if he knew this was coming. I kind of wish I would've had a chance to kiss him, just for practice, before we have to do it in front of the camera.

"Is that alright?" Dex says.

I shake my head and turn my head back to him.

"Yeah… yeah, it's fine… of course."

He smiles at me. I can tell he's still trying to decide if he's convinced by my answer, but I don't know what else I could have said. I have a feeling tonight is going to be a long night and I probably won't sleep well. Jess is going to be excited though. It's exactly what she wants for me.

I force thoughts of kissing Spencer out of my mind. There's going to be plenty of time to be a worried mess tomorrow.

Hopefully I do a convincing job of kissing him. More than anything I don't want to disappoint Dex and I know the kiss has to look real, otherwise the audience will never believe it.

"I know that I probably should have mentioned it before… it's not something I even thought about until yesterday. I… I knew it was in the movie, obviously, but I hadn't even considered it since we cast you."

"It's fine… really, Dex, I don't mind."

He chuckles, takes his phone out his pocket and checks something before turning his attention back to me.

"You know, most girls your age would be thrilled… but I know that you're not most girls and that's why you're in my movie."

I think that was a compliment....

"Thanks."

Dex stands up, starts walking toward the house and I follow. He holds the door open for me and I go inside.

"I've gotta make a few calls," he says. "Dinner at six?"

"Sure."

He smiles and heads toward the kitchen. I climb the stairs and go to my room. I could do with a few hours to myself. Not to mention, I have to start psyching myself up for tomorrow's kiss. I wonder if Spencer knows about this already? He must.

I lie down on my bed and try to calm my pulse and breathing. I remind myself to not dwell on the things I can't change and instead focus on the positives... like the fact that I should be able to get back to Salem for the start of school.

CHAPTER SIXTEEN

"Are you ready?" Dex says.

I feel like I'm about to die. No... I'm not ready. Not at all.

"Yes... I think so."

"Good. Just try to be natural... it has to look convincing. When he leans in to kiss you, I want you to look into his eyes... look into his soul. I want you to look like you understand every fiber of his being and then... then I want you to kiss him with every molecule of passion in your body."

Well... at least he's not putting any pressure on me. I close my eyes and try to even out my breathing. My heart is beating so fast I'm sure that everyone in the building can hear it. I really believe that nothing in my life up to this point has prepared me for this moment... the moment I kiss Spencer Thomas and it's recorded for the world to see.

I take a deep breath and nod.

"I'm ready."

"Good," Dex says.

He retreats to behind the camera and flashes me a smile. I suddenly feel alone... alone in a room full of people. There must be forty people here—all looking at me and standing at least ten feet away. It's a very weird feeling, something I don't think I can even put into words other than it's making me uneasy.

Spencer walks onto the set and every head in the room, including mine, turns to look at him. He looks as perfect as ever and it's hard not to stare. He walks up to me and smiles. The sadness in his eyes from yesterday is gone, replaced by the same swagger he usually sports.

"Good morning," he says.

"Hi."

"Are you ready to make out?"

There's a humorous tone to his voice, which actually goes a long way in making me feel less nervous. He obviously knows what he's doing and I have a feeling this isn't his first time kissing a very nervous girl in front of a group of what essentially amounts to strangers.

"Are you OK?"

I open my mouth to answer, but no words come out. Spencer smiles and leans his mouth close to my ear.

"There's nothing to be afraid of… you're going to be amazing, just like with everything else you do. It's going to be over in a matter of seconds and then you'll laugh at yourself for ever being nervous about it… I promise."

He takes my hand in his and squeezes it as he pulls his head back.

"Thanks."

I feel a little better, not amazing, but certainly a little calmer. Spencer having faith in me, in addition to Dex, reminds me that they wanted me here… they know what they're doing and they wouldn't have asked me to be in the movie if they didn't think I could handle everything they threw my way.

They have complete trust in me. It's time for me to start trusting them.

"Are you ready?" Dex says.

Spencer looks at me and I nod. I'm as ready as I'm ever

going to be.

"Yeah… we're ready," Spencer says, calling over his shoulder.

"Quiet on the set! Action!"

I try to remember exactly what Dex said to me about kissing Spencer, but the moment I look into his eyes it's all gone… my mind is blank and the only thing I can think about is the gorgeous man standing in front of me.

He looks into my eyes and I feel something new… it's a spark, deep inside of me. It's different, in a good way, from anything else I've known in my life. I look into his eyes and even if it's for just a brief moment in time, I feel like there's nothing more I want than to kiss Spencer… I need to kiss him.

It's a crazy feeling… something that I've never experienced before—not with Mitch or Logan, not on this level at least. It's like my body knows something that my brain doesn't.

Spencer lowers his head and presses his lips against mine. I feel an intense heat building deep in my chest before it explodes and shoots through every inch of my body. It fills me with a sense of ultimate happiness as a soft moan escapes my lips. The whole world around me, the cameras and everyone watching, fades and I lose myself completely in Spencer.

I feel Spencer wrap his arm around my waist as he pulls me closer and his tongue passes into my mouth. My own tongue darts out and touches his. I never want this moment to end.

"Cut," Dex says.

I don't stop kissing Spencer and he doesn't pull away from me. He groans as I thrust my tongue into his mouth and he moves his hand from my waist to my ass. Spencer squeezes my butt and I can feel my feet leave the ground briefly as he lifts me up. We finally break our kiss and look into each other's eyes. His gaze feels like a thousand suns beating down on me and I melt. Spencer catches me before I fall over.

"Cut!"

We finally turn to Dex, who is still standing next to the camera. I'm not sure how to describe the look on his face... maybe shock. I see the same look on everyone's face as I look around the room.

"How was that?" Spencer says.

No one in the room moves and I suddenly realize they are all staring at me. I feel my face turn bright red as I realize I've just shared what felt like an incredibly intimate moment with a room full of people I really don't know.

Dex doesn't even get a chance to answer Spencer before I put my hands over my face and run. I think I hear my name as I make it out of the building, but I don't turn around. I'm out of breath as I reach my trailer. I go inside and lock the door behind me. I collapse on the couch and wipe the first tears from my eyes just as they form.

I can't believe that just happened. It was embarrassing enough, just having people watching, but the fact that it was so intense is what made it worse. It felt so real to me, but I'm sure to Spencer it was just a part of the job. I'm such an idiot. I should have known something like this would have happened.

There's a knock on my door and I freeze.

"Amy?"

I breathe a sigh of relief. It's Dex. I was worried it would be Spencer. I don't think I can even look at him right now, it might kill me. He tries the door and then knocks again.

"Amy, are you in there?"

I take a deep breath and clear my throat before answering.

"Yeah."

"Can I come in?"

I really just want to curl up into a ball and pretend like I'm alone in the world—it would be less painful than the reality of what just happened, but he's my boss and I still have to go to his house at the end of the day.

"One second."

I grab a tissue and dab my eyes to get the tears before they roll down my cheek and I unlock the door. Dex opens it and comes in. He smiles at me and points at the couch. We both walk over and sit down before he says a word.

"Are you alright?"

I shrug. No, I'm not... I just know that I can't say anything. Not to mention, I feel like I'm making a big deal out of what is probably nothing to the rest of the people who witnessed my kiss with Spencer.

"You can talk to me, really... you can tell me anything, Amy."

I look at Dex and I can tell he's willing to listen and not judge me, but still... I'm scared to tell him, or anyone, what I'm feeling right now. I'm not even really sure what I'm thinking other than the fact that I'm embarrassed.

"I... I'm sorry for running off like that."

Dex nods and looks at me. I expected him to admonish me for running off the set, but he has a kind look in his eyes, like no matter what I say he's not going to judge me.

"I don't know... it was... hard. It was hard to do that scene."

"Why?"

I shrug.

"Was it all the people watching?"

"Not really. I'm not sure what it was."

"Amy, you can tell me anything... I'm your friend, not just your director."

I've felt like our relationship ran deeper than just work, but it's still nice to hear the words coming from his mouth.

"I... I don't know if I can really explain it," I say.

"Just try."

I close my eyes and try corralling every thought that's running through my mind. I want to tell Dex what's really going on... I'm just worried that he might not understand, that he might think it's stupid and he will think less of me. I guess that's a risk I have to take because he seems like he's not going to leave until I tell him what it is.

"It's Spencer... I've... I don't know, Dex, I'm not sure how to even explain it.... The other night, the night I spent at his house, we went out to a club and I had a couple of drinks, on accident, and when we got back to his house I tried to kiss him. I'm not sure why I tried, other than maybe because that's what pretty much every girl wants that looks at him."

I look back at Dex, expecting him to... I'm not sure what, but I wasn't expecting him to have a smile on his face.

"You're not the first, and I'm sure you won't be the last, girl or woman to feel a strong pull to Spencer. He... he has an intangible quality to affect those around him."

I nod. Dex is right. Spencer certainly does... I just didn't think I'd ever fall for that. I guess I was wrong.

"I don't know... it was just weird. And then I went with him to Colorado, which was fine, but right as were leaving, he brought up the fact that his mom thought we were dating and he didn't have the heart to tell her the truth. He got emotional and didn't talk to me, pretty much, until today. I don't know, it's just weird."

Dex sighs and nods. I can tell by the look on his face that he knows the reason for what Spencer did and he's not about to tell me.

"Give him a chance to tell you himself."

"But what do I do now? That kiss... I don't know... it just made me feel so many things."

Dex laughs and stands up from the couch.

"I don't know what to tell you about that... you're going to have to figure out that all by yourself. Only you know how you feel. I can tell you, though, that in all my years in this business I've never seen such a convincing kiss... and I've worked with husbands and wives."

Dex smiles at me again as I sit there in shock. Did he

just say what I think he did? He walks out of my trailer and I'm alone, again, with my thoughts. Dex didn't say anything about getting back to the set, so I'm not even really sure what I'm supposed to be doing right now. I know we have a couple more scenes to shoot today. The longer I wait to go back, the worse it is. Everyone is just waiting for me.

I stand up and go to the bathroom. It's fortunate, what little makeup I had on this morning wasn't disturbed by the tears as I managed to stop them in time.

"You can do this," I say, looking into my own eyes in the mirror. "Spencer sees you as a co-worker… everything is all about doing the job well and making Dex proud with the final product. I can do anything he can."

CHAPTER SEVENTEEN

"Cut!" Dex says.

I turn to Spencer and he smiles as everyone starts to clap.

"That's a wrap!"

It's kind of hard to believe it's over. Dex said he thought we could finish early and he was right. School doesn't start for ten days. We may be done shooting, but he said he's been making some calls, trying to get us an interview of some kind to start building some buzz around the movie.

From what Spencer has told me, shooting a movie this quickly pretty much never happens, but he said Dex has been really smart about shooting... that and he pretty much hasn't stopped working, day or night, for the last few weeks.

Dex walks over to us. He smiles at me and wraps his arms around me in a soft hug, reminiscent of my dad hugging me when I was younger.

"Thank you," he says, whispering into my ear.

He lets me go and hugs Spencer.

"Let's go celebrate," Dex says.

"I just have to go back to my trailer and change," I say.

Dex waves the idea off.

"No time, I need a drink, and there's already a car waiting for us."

I laugh and shake my head as Spencer and I follow Dex to the parking lot. It's been a rough couple weeks... I never imagined working on a movie would be this much work and I'm glad it's over, but I'm also a little disappointed that my time here is coming to an end.

We get to the parking lot and climb in the waiting limo as the rest of the production crew and cast gets in their own cars. I feel a little bad, like I'm getting the royal treatment... like I'm somehow more important than them.

"So," Dex says, as the limo starts to pull out of the lot, "I got you two a spot on Late with Lucas, in five days. I know it's a little last minute, one of their guests dropped out. I've got a jet reserved for tomorrow at ten, so try to take it easy tonight."

I don't plan on having anything to drink, so that won't be a problem for me. I'm kind of excited to be going on a TV show... it's another thing I never imagined I would ever do. I've heard of Late with Lucas, but I've never actually seen it.

"Where are we going?" I say.

I know it's kind of a stupid question, but I'm curious and I have a feeling neither of them is going to mention it if I don't ask.

"New York," Dex says.

Wow. I've always thought it would be fun to visit and it sounds like we might be there for a few days before we actually have to do the interview... I hope that we can do some touristy stuff. I know New York is probably old hat for Spencer and Dex, but the idea of going is exciting to me.

"Where's the wrap party?" Spencer says.

"It's at some art gallery... I've never been there, but a friend of a friend owns the place and suggested it."

"Oh, nice."

I look out the window and lose myself in the passing buildings as Spencer and Dex talk. I guess I'm going to spend my birthday in New York. That should be fun. I'll have to head to school after that. It seems like the shortest summer of my life... I know for sure it's been the most eventful. I'm definitely looking forward to seeing Jess though, I really miss her.

The limo comes to a stop and the driver climbs out to get our door. Spencer gets out, followed by Dex and me last. I look up at the sign of the gallery that says *GLOW* in red letters, lit by spotlights that are sitting on the street. It looks... modern. The doorman opens the door and we head inside. We are the first ones and I look around at some of the art while Dex and Spencer head over to the bar.

"Do you want anything, Amy?" Spencer says.

"No, thanks."

I walk up to a painting and stare at it, trying to figure out what it's supposed to be. I guess modern art is supposed to be open to more liberal interpretation, but I have no idea what this even reminds me of. It looks like someone just smeared red paint over ninety percent of a white canvas. I would hardly call it art, but I guess someone must like it.

"I'm going to miss you."

I turn my head and see Spencer standing to my right and just behind me. I don't think he was there long, but I didn't hear him walking over.

"I... I'll miss you, too."

"Do you have to leave?" he says.

It's kind of a weird question... we've formed a friendship, of sorts, and we got along fine while working together, but I haven't really given much thought to the reality that once I head back to Salem I'll probably never see him again.

A sad thought, for sure, but I have to start the rest of my life. There's really nothing here for me. Despite the constant reinforcement and positive feedback about my acting from both Spencer and Dex, I know I don't have a future in it... and I'm not sure that's something I would even want.

"Yes."

I turn my attention back to the art and move down the wall to the next painting. It looks almost exactly the same as the first, but this time it's blue. I look under the painting and read the tag. It says *Blue by Henric Alvans, $2799*. I feel like they might have forgotten the decimal point.

Spencer puts his hand on my shoulder and gives it a light squeeze.

"If... if you... I... never mind," he says.

What could he possibly want to say that he could have that much trouble with? I turn to face Spencer, but his back is to me and he's walking toward the front door where the crew and other actors and starting to walk in.

I know Spencer is a complicated guy, more than most people who watch his movies would ever know, but I'm not about to press him to speak up about what he's thinking... I don't want to put that kind of pressure on him. I think there's a darker side to him that people don't see... the side that I caught a glimpse of after our trip. I wonder what could cause a person so much pain.

I walk down the wall until I find something that isn't monochromatic. I finally find one, tucked in a dark back corner with just a single light shining on the middle of it. I'm still not sure what it's supposed to be, but I feel like leaving a painting up to interpretation is a part of modern art. The yellow is so vibrant that I can feel the warmth coming off the painting. The greens remind me of grass and it's almost like I can smell it... that fresh cut grass smell.

"Hey."

I turn and see Rodger, the assistant director, standing next to me.

"Hi."

"What do you think of that painting?"

"It's… I love it. It makes me feel like I'm standing in a field of freshly cut grass and looking up in the sky as the sun warms my face."

He smiles at me and walks off. I wonder what that was about. I look under the painting, at the tag. It says *Morning by Rodger Weiss, $1975*. I smile and shake my head. I'm glad that he painted it because Rodger is a great guy and he was really helpful during the shoot when I needed some direction and wasn't quite getting what Dex was saying. It's funny because it seemed like Rodger always had a simple way of explaining things, but I can see by the painting that he's much more complex than he leads on.

I make a loop around the rest of the gallery and end up at the front, where Dex is talking to a man I've never seen before. I start to walk by them, not wanting to interrupt, but Dex turns to me and motions for me to join them.

"Amy, I want you to meet Nathan Poll."

He holds his hand out and we shake. I'm a little surprised he's here… I thought it was just cast and crew.

"Nice to meet you," he says. "If you did half as well as Dex said I have a feeling we are all in for a real treat."

"Sorry?" I say.

"I was telling Nathan about the film," Dex says.

I nod and smile. I'm not sure what Dex could have told him that would suggest I did a good job, especially since we just wrapped today.

"Well," I say, "I hope that it lives up to your expectations. Dex did an amazing job of trying to mold me into an actress in a short amount of time."

"Have you seen Spencer?" Dex says.

"Yeah… I just talked to him, but I'm not sure where he is now."

I look around the room, but I don't see him anywhere. This place isn't that big and he's usually not that hard to spot in a room full of people.

"Let's go find him," Dex says, talking to Nathan.

143

"It was nice to meet you, Amy."

"You too, Nathan."

He smiles at me and follows Dex into the crowd of people in search of Spencer. Hopefully my conversation with Spencer didn't cause him to leave. I doubt that it would, but I guess it's a possibility because I don't see him anywhere.

I look around the room at everyone that's become part of my life since I've been here. Pretty much everyone is here and I'm glad because it seems like a farewell party... I'll never see these people again. It's weird to think that, after seeing them every day for the last couple months, but it's true.

Leslie, who did my hair and makeup, walks up to me and puts her arms around me and manages to not spill her drink in the process.

"Amy, I'm going to miss you."

I smile as she breaks our hug.

"I'll miss you, too."

"So, what's next for you?"

"School."

She nods and forces a smile. I can tell she's not excited at all about the prospect of college.

"That'll be... interesting."

"Yeah, I'm looking forward to it."

Dex walks up to us and stands next to Leslie.

"Did you find Spencer?" I say.

"Nope... but someone said they saw him leaving and that he looked upset."

"Weird."

I hope that I didn't have anything to do with it.

"Yeah... unusual behavior for him," Dex says. "He's not one to leave a party early."

Dex is right. Now I feel like I should have never said anything about telling his mom the truth about our relationship because I think it's still weighing on his mind and it's all my fault. If he brings it up again... I don't know what I'll even say, but I'll support whatever he thinks is best. I don't want to upset his mom.

"His loss," Dex says. "Now, I need to find another drink… Leslie, would you care to accompany in that quest?"

"I would love that."

I watch as they walk off toward the makeshift bar. I'm really going to miss him. He's really been more than I could have ever hoped for and I hope that I did him proud with my acting.

CHAPTER EIGHTEEN

I sit down on my bed and pick up my phone, the second phone Dex has given me. I promised to take better care of this one and not break it, like the last one, but he waved his hand and told me it wasn't a big deal. I'm not sure that I would ever get used to this kind of life… where something like a phone that costs hundreds of dollars is practically disposable, but I'm going to miss all of this.

There's a text from Jess waiting for me.

Hey, just got your text. That's so exciting! How's New York? Is your room nice?

I look around the hotel room. Nice is one way of describing it. I think breathtaking is more appropriate… but I would describe it as inspiring. I stand up and walk over to the window and look at Central Park. A view that I would never tire of.

It's amazing. I'm looking out a floor-to-ceiling window at Central Park. It's jaw dropping. I never imagined that a city could look this beautiful. I don't ever want to leave. And the room… it's something else. It's not huge, not a suite or anything, but everything is really nice and I'm sure it was really expensive.

I hit send and turn the desk chair to face the window and sit down. The sun is going down and starting to hit the glass of the buildings that cover the skyline. It's beautiful. People can make such magnificent things… impressive in a completely different way than nature. Maybe that's why this view is so divine… there's the buildings and the park… a perfect balance of the creations of nature and man.

Ugh. I'm so jelly. Take some pictures for me! I wish I were there with you… we could find some trouble in that city.

I laugh at her text. There's no doubt in my mind that Jess would manage to get us both into trouble if she were here.

Already did… I'll send them to you right now.

I go to my pictures, but phone starts to ring and Spencer's number shows up. I take a deep breath and answer it.

"Hello?"

"Hey," he says, "what are you doing?"

"Nothing… just sitting here, looking at the park."

"It's something else, isn't it?"

It's weird… Spencer's voice seems shaky, almost like he's nervous or something.

"Yeah, it is. Did you need something?" I say.

He's quiet, which for some odd reasons is making me nervous.

"Spencer?"

"Sorry… I… can you come up to my room for a minute? I have something I need to talk to you about."

I pull my phone away from my ear to check the time. We have to leave in twenty minutes.

"Yeah, but you've gotta make it quick… we have to leave soon."

"I know, it'll just take a few minutes," he says.

"I'll be right there."

When we checked in yesterday I went to see both Dex and Spencer's suites, which are much nicer than my regular room. I have a feeling they paid some exorbitant amount of money for them without even thinking about it. It was nice of Dex to pay for my room, though... I guess it makes sense since we are here to promote the movie.

I stand up, put my phone in my purse and check to make sure I have my room key before heading to meet Spencer. I get in the elevator and ride the three flights up to their floor and get out.

Spencer's door is propped open with a shoe, so I push it away and close the door behind me.

"Spencer?"

I walk deeper into his room and see him standing at the window. His view faces the same way as mine, but being higher up makes it even more impressive. He turns around and smiles.

"Can I get you anything to drink?"

He has a glass in his hand filled with a brown liquid.

"No, thanks."

I still haven't had anything to drink since the night at the club. I don't want to make a fool of myself again and especially not around Spencer. He shrugs and turns back to the window.

"What did you need to talk about? We have like fifteen minutes before we need to leave," I say.

"There's something on the table for you."

I wrinkle my brow as I look at the table and see two boxes. One is flat and the other looks like a shoe box. I walk over and take the lid off the smaller box. Inside is a pair of shoes, black and beautiful. I run my hand over the soft material, which feels like suede. They are crisscross platform sandals with a fairly significant heel, maybe five inches or so.

"What do you think?" Spencer says.

I turn to him with one of the shoes in my hand. He's still at the window, but he's facing me and smiling. I'm sure he can tell what I think by the look on my face.

"I love them. You really shouldn't have... they must have been expensive."

He waves his hand dismissively and walks over to me.

"Whatever... it's an investment in your future. Don't forget, we're going to be on TV... if people like what they see they will go to our movie and then we make more money."

It's a valid point, but I don't think it would make that much of a difference. I'm wearing an outfit I borrowed from the movie set, so it's something my character might wear, but it's certainly not designer like the shoes.

"They're Alexander McQueen," he says, "to match the dress."

The dress? I feel my heart skip a beat. I may be from a small town, but I've heard of Alexander McQueen and I know enough to know that it's a name that means expensive.

I put the shoe down on the table and yank the lid off the box. I gasp and reach for the dress. I spin around, stand in front of the floor length mirror and hold the dress up. It's stunning... I can't even believe that Spencer did this for me. It's a sleeveless flared skirt dress, with a low neckline and it ends a few inches above my knees. I'm speechless.

"What do you think?"

Spencer is standing behind me, to get a good look. His warm breath sweeps my hair off my neck and I shudder. I close my eyes as I feel his breath warming me. If only this moment could never end. I really haven't thought about Spencer, not seriously, since our one and only kiss, but now... now I wish he would spin me around and smash his lips onto mine. I know it would never happen though, which makes me sad... but a girl can dream.

"I guess you're speechless."

That's one way to put it.

I turn around and look into his gorgeous eyes and nearly lose myself.

"It's... too much, Spencer. You really shouldn't have."

He turns and walks over to the couch and sits down. Spencer takes his phone out of his pocket and looks at it while I turn back to the mirror and hold the dress up again. It really is stunning. I'm a little worried about how low the neckline is, but I trust Spencer's judgment when it comes to clothing.

"You should change… we need to be downstairs in five minutes. We can't be late for Late with Lucas, ironically enough," he says.

"I don't get it… why do we have to be there soon? I mean, I know the sun is going down, but doesn't it air at like ten, or something?"

"Yep, but it's not live."

I guess that makes sense, if they filmed it live the audience might be tired and the guests could appear fatigued or something. I look at myself one last time and dash to the bathroom to get changed.

I take my clothes off and toss them on the counter in the bathroom and slip into the dress. It fits perfectly… well nearly, but I can't seem to get the zipper up and I don't want to break it. I'm surprised Spencer remembered my size because it's like this dress was made for me. I head back into the room, with my hand behind my back to hold it up.

"What's wrong?"

"Nothing… it's amazing, but I can't zip it up. Could you help me?"

He raises his eyebrow and hops up. I hope he doesn't think I'm just saying that I can't get it. I realize that it's super cliché, the girl can't get her dress up or down and has to ask the handsome guy to help her and it always leads to something. This isn't the movies, and I wouldn't ask for help, but I'm scared of ruining the dress.

He stands behind me and I feel his fingers brush against my back as he grabs the zipper. I feel like time slows as he zips it up. It must be my mind wishing for the moment to last because as soon as he's done he steps back in front of me and looks me up and down.

"Perfect."

I look at the floor. I know he's just looking to make sure it fits me, but having his eyes roam my body makes me feel embarrassed. I know I don't compare physically to pretty much every woman in Hollywood, but I like the way I look in the dress.

"Hurry, get your shoes on… Dex is probably already waiting for us."

I nod and walk over to the table. I put my left hand on the back of the chair as I put my right shoe on and then switch. As I put my weight on the back of the chair with my right hand I feel it falling backward.

"Ahhh!"

I close my eyes and brace for the impact I know is coming. Instead, I feel a hand under my back and an arm wrap around my waist and by the time I open my eyes Spencer is already putting me back on my feet. I blink a few times to make sure what I think just happened really did.

"Thank you… that was… amazing."

He laughs and kneels on the floor to help me with my shoe. That's the second time I've fallen and he's been there to catch me. Crazy.

"No problem."

He stands up and smiles at me. Spencer knows he's a superhero and I'm not about to build up his ego any more. Not that I wouldn't, under normal circumstances… I'm just afraid that he might get the wrong idea and I don't want that right before we go on a talk show together to promote the film.

"Ready?"

"I am."

He winks at me and we leave his hotel room. Spencer pats his pocket to check for his key and closes the door. I press the elevator button and focus on keeping equal weight on each foot. I haven't worn heels since the party with Jess and I've forgotten how much of a challenge it is. I definitely don't want to take a spill while walking…

Emma Keene

Spencer would probably laugh at me.

"What are you thinking about?" he says.

"Nothing... why?"

"Oh, no reason... you just had a determined kind of look on your face."

The elevator dings and the doors open. We step in and Spencer hits the lobby button.

"So," he says, "do you ever watch Late with Lucas?"

"Nope, never seen it."

The elevator slows and the doors open after only going down two floors. A couple decked to the nines gets in. It's obvious by their demeanor they've already been pre-gaming in their room and are ready to hit the town.

"Are you guys going to the club?" the man says, turning around and looking at us.

The woman turns around, too, and her eyes go wide when she recognizes Spencer. It's starting to just be funny when people realize who he is. I'm glad that it'll never happen to me, I don't think I would be as nice as Spencer... he's always grateful that people enjoy his movies and always willing to sign an autograph.

"Oh... my... god! Spencer Thomas! Eeeeeeeeeeee!" she says.

I think I might be deaf. I look over at Spencer and he's just smiling.

"Hey," he says.

"What are you doing here?"

"We," Spencer says, nodding to me, "are going on Late with Lucas... we've got a new movie coming out, so we are going to do some promotion."

The couple turns to me and stares. They seem like they are trying their best to place my face. I guess they think if I'm with Spencer that I must be famous, too.

"I'm... nobody," I say.

They seem disappointed, as if I'm lying to them, and turn their attention back to Spencer.

"Can we buy you a drink or something? The bar here is

great."

"Thanks," Spencer says, "but we are actually running late. Maybe some other time."

The couple smiles and nods. Spencer is so gracious. I know it's true that we are running late, but it was more than that... I know him well enough that he's not going to hang out with some random drunk people he meets in a hotel elevator, but he doesn't come across that way.

We reach the lobby and the doors open. The couple gets out and we follow. I can see Dex standing by the door, looking at his phone and probably wondering where we are. His eyes grow wide as he looks up and sees us. Spencer and I walk up to him and he looks me up and down.

"Nice... nice outfit."

"Thanks."

I can feel myself blushing and I look down at my feet.

"Should we go?" Spencer says.

"Yeah," Dex says, "there's a car waiting out front."

He looks at me again and shakes his head. Not in a disapproving way... no, it's more of a surprised look that flashes across his face. Do I really look that different? I like the dress and shoes, but I don't think I ever look that great... I guess it's just how I see myself, so it's a new experience for anyone to see me as a woman instead of just a girl from a small town.

We head for the door and the doorman smiles as we walk outside. It's weird, but I suddenly feel like people are noticing me. I don't really mind, I'm more surprised than anything. There's a black limo out front and the driver opens the door as he sees us walking toward him. I get in first and slide across the seat to the window. Dex gets in, followed by Spencer and they both sit across from me.

I stare out the window as they start talking to each other. It's not that I would mind being a part of the conversation, I just feel like I want to be alone with my thoughts right now.

A strange sadness has filled me. I'm not really sure why either. I thought I'd be happy to be here, doing the promo for the movie, because it means we are done and I get to go back to Salem... but I'm not. Instead, I'm profoundly sad and it doesn't make sense. I feel like now I'm realizing that leaving L.A. doesn't just mean that I get to go back to Salem—it also means that I have to leave L.A. and the semblance of a life I've built there in a short time. I haven't been there for very long, but I also wasn't in Salem for any amount of time. It's weird, I almost feel like... like I don't know where I'm supposed to be. I guess school is the most important thing right now.

CHAPTER NINETEEN

"Are you ready?" Spencer says, whispering into my ear.

I nod, not even bothering to talk… between the clapping of the audience and the music I don't think he would even be able to hear me.

I look at Spencer, to see if he's going to go on stage first, but he holds out his hand. I take a deep breath and walk out. I turn toward the audience, which is maybe two hundred people, and wave to them while trying my best to not squint with the massive amount of lights that are shining in my eyes.

They clap and make noise, but I can tell the moment when Spencer steps onto the stage because everyone goes crazy.

There are two black chairs next to the desk of Lucas. He stands up as we walk toward him. He's dressed sharply, a gray suit with a white shirt and a dark blue skinny tie. Lucas holds his hand out and shakes mine first and then Spencer's. We sit down, me in the chair next to the desk and Spencer on my right. I pick up a glass of water from the coffee table and take a drink while we wait for the crowd to settle.

"So," Lucas says, "Amy, Spencer, thanks for being

here."

"Thanks for having us," we say.

"My pleasure. Spencer, what have you been up to? I heard you split with your longtime girlfriend, Monica Lister... is it true?"

I'm a little surprised that this is the first question... I guess people care more about drama and celebrity gossip than the film we made.

"Yes, but that's not why *we* are here... *we* are here to talk about our new film."

Lucas looks surprised by the directness of the answer and nods. He must have been expecting Spencer to try and dodge the question.

"Fair enough," Lucas says. "Amy, how was working with Dexter Baldwin, say, compared to other directors you've worked with."

"Um, well, this is my first film... so I really have nothing to compare it to, but Dex is amazing. He had a beautiful vision for what he wanted, so we did our best to make good on that."

His eyes go wide and blinks a few times while looking at me, almost like he's still trying to process the fact that I was cast as the female lead in an award winning director's film my first time out. I get that it's a little crazy for me, but I'm sure it's not the first time it's happened.

"OK... Spencer, how did Amy do?"

Lucas's voice is a little shaky, suggesting this isn't anywhere close to where he thought this interview would go and he's not sure what to talk about.

"She... she was amazing. I can't give her enough praise for the job she did."

The audience claps briefly.

"When is the movie coming out?"

"Well," Spencer says, "Dex has been hard at work editing with his team and it should be ready in a couple of weeks... but as for when it's coming out, that I don't know. The plan, as far as I know, is that it's going to hit the festival circuit and I guess after that... I'm not sure, sorry... that's a question for Dex."

"We'll make sure to keep an eye out for it, when it does hit theaters. We have a clip from the film," Lucas says. "Does one of you want to set it up?'

I turn to Spencer. Dex didn't mention anything to me about showing a clip, so I have no idea what it is.

"Sure, Lucas. This is the point in the film where the characters finally admit, to themselves and each other, their feelings. It was an emotional journey to this point and they find solace when they finally decide to be together."

Oh, no. Are we about to watch what I think we are?

"Great, let's go ahead and roll it."

We all turn our attention to the large screen behind us and watch as the clips rolls. Crap. It's exactly what I thought... it's the kiss.

I wish I could close my eyes and when I open them be back home, in Greenville, and none of this will have ever happened.

I'm not sure why I'm so worked up, really... this is what I signed up for when I agreed to be in the movie. Yeah, I didn't know that I would have to kiss Spencer and I knew people would see whatever I did, but it's still scary to be sitting in front of a room full of people watching it and knowing millions could see it. Maybe I'll get lucky and the world will end before this airs.

I know I'm being silly, but there's something intimate about a kiss, even when it's being filmed. I open my eyes as the clip ends and I turn back around. The audience is quiet, silent really. Spencer and I turn to Lucas, who just keeps blinking... not saying anything.

"That," he says, "that... was... I don't even know how to explain it other than saying it was... it was perfect."

He shakes his head and turns back to the audience. They start clapping, even louder than when they saw Spencer. It feels unreal to be sitting here and having this many people impressed by something Spencer and I did. I get that Dex was happy with the kiss, but this is something entirely different.

The audience finally starts to settle down and Lucas turns his attention to the camera straight in front of him.

"We're going to take a quick commercial break… don't go anywhere."

A young guy comes running onto the stage and refills our water glasses. I pick mine up and take another drink. I feel like I'm in a state of shock, or something right now… nothing feels real. Is this really me?

"Spencer?" Lucas says.

"Yeah?"

"I was planning to ask you more about Monica, but I can see that you don't feel the need…. Would you mind if I asked Amy a few questions instead?"

Spencer laughs and turns to me.

"You should be asking her, not me."

Lucas turns to me and waits for my answer.

"I… sure, I don't see why not," I say.

"Ten seconds!" someone says, from off stage.

Lucas looks over a page of notes on his desk and nods before turning his attention back to the camera directly in front of him. I watch as the cameraman gives him a thumbs up.

"Welcome back to Late with Lucas. So, Amy," he says, turning to me, "tell us about yourself… where are you from? How old are you? All that fun stuff, if you don't mind."

"Sure, Lucas. Well, I'm from a small town called Greenville, that no one has ever heard of… so that's not really all that exciting."

"Is that why you ended up in Hollywood? Small town couldn't contain you any longer?"

I glance over at Spencer as I try to think of how to even answer that. I'm not about to go that deep into my personal life on national TV.

"Yeah, Lucas… something like that."

"And how old are you?"

"I just turned eighteen two days ago, three days after we wrapped on the film."

"Happy late birthday," he says.

"Thanks."

"How does it feel to finally be... legal."

I wrinkle my forehead as the audience laughs. I have a pretty good idea what he's implying and I don't really like it. I see Lucas look by me, to Spencer, and he swallows and turns his attention to the papers on his desk.

"Umm... so, Amy, I guess... well, can you tell us what film you're working on next?"

I take a deep breath. I want to refuse to answer him and walk off the stage right now... the longer his comment has to sink in the worse I feel about it, but I remind myself that Dex and Spencer are both counting on me. I can stick it out for a couple more minutes and finish this interview for their sake.

"I've got nothing planned... I'm actually heading to college this week, it's about to start. I don't have any plans to do any more acting... this was kind of a one time thing for me."

Lucas looks shocked and stares at me.

"Seriously?"

"Yes... seriously."

I'm not sure what he's trying to imply, but I don't think I like it. He's starting to really irritate me.

"How did you end up getting cast in the film?"

I decide to skip the part of the story that involves my mom.

"Well, I was working as Dex's personal assistant and they were trying to cast for the film and didn't seem happy with any of the girls that were coming in to read. Spencer asked me to read the script, out loud, and so I did. I didn't realize it at the time, but he had convinced Dex to let me audition. That's kind of it."

"Wow... well, that just goes to show everyone out

there that you never know when you'll get your big break in life."

Lucas forces a smile on his face and turns back to the camera. I'm glad this is over because I don't know how much longer I can pretend to tolerate him.

"One last commercial break before our last guest of the night... who is it? You'll have to come back to see... but I'll give you a hint—if you're a sports fan, you're not going to want to miss this."

The same young guy runs out onto stage and refills our waters again. I start to stand up, but Spencer puts his hand on my arm. I turn to him and flash him a confused look. He leans close to me.

"We are supposed to stay while his next guest is on, that's how this show works."

I sit back down and fold my arms across my body. I was really hoping to get out of here as soon as possible. I guess I don't have much of a choice. I take a deep breath and close my eyes as I try to calm myself down.

The water guy comes back with another chair and sets it down on the other side of the desk. I guess the other guest will be sitting over there. Hopefully it'll limit the interaction I have with them because I'm not much of a sports fan at all.

Lucas turns back to the camera and flashes another fake smile. Ugh.

"Welcome back to Late with Lucas... my last guest of the night is... well, if you're a sports fan, he doesn't need any introduction... please welcome the number one college football prospect heading into this season... Logan Reynolds!!!"

My heart sinks. Is this a bad dream? There's no way this can really be happening right now.

I look to the other side of the stage and I see Logan walking toward us, his head is turned toward the audience and he's waving. He turns toward Lucas and stops cold. We lock eyes and I see anger building on his face as he notices Spencer next to me.

It takes everything in me to not jump up and run off the stage... that and Spencer has his hand on my arm. He leans over and I feel his breath against my neck.

"Don't let him get to you... what happened between you had nothing to do with you... it was all his own doing. Be the bigger, better person that I know you are, Amy."

I'm glad that one of us has some confidence in me.

Logan shakes Lucas's hand and sits down, I look away and into the bright lights hanging above the crowd... at this point I'll take being blind over having to look at Logan.

"So, Logan, how are you?"

Logan doesn't respond right away... I have a feeling he's in the same state of shock that's making me feel paralyzed right now. I'm just glad my interview is done and I can kind of just sit here because I can't imagine being in his shoes right now—especially since he believes that I was fooling around on him with Spencer... Logan has to be fuming right now.

"Logan?" Lucas says.

"What's *she* doing here?"

"Sorry?"

"Why is Amy here?"

"Um... she's a guest. Do you know her or something?"

The audience is silent as they wait in heightened anticipation. I'm sure they weren't expecting this.

"You could say that," Logan says.

"Really? Where do you know her from?"

I can tell by the tone of Lucas's voice that he's doing his best to push Logan over the edge. Lucas wants nothing more than to see him explode because he knows it'll be good for ratings... and frankly, I find that insulting and offensive that I'm being forced to be a part of this.

I stand up and walk off the stage. Spencer doesn't try to stop me this time and when I glance over my shoulder he's only a few steps behind me. I stop and turn once we are off stage and I rip my mic off and toss it on the floor. Spencer does the same and we start walking again. We head back to the green room and I sit down on the couch. Dex is there, waiting for us. I look up and see a TV that's showing live what's happened and notice that Logan's not on stage and Lucas seems to be panicking. Good.

"I... I'm so sorry," I say.

I can feel tears starting to well in my eyes. I think there's a part of me that misses Logan more than I realize and seeing him again has brought those feelings crashing back... that and I wasn't enjoying being made into a freak show by some rude talk show host. Dex gets up, sits next to me and looks into my eyes.

"Don't ever apologize for being you... I didn't like how Lucas was interviewing you and bringing Logan out made it even worse. I don't blame you for leaving. I would've done the same, but I don't think I would have even stayed as long as you did."

"I... I didn't want to let you down."

Dex starts to laugh.

"Please, you could never disappoint me... you're amazing in so many ways. If I had a daughter, I would want her to be you."

That does it. The tears start to stream down my cheeks and Dex wraps his arms around me and gives me the hug I so desperately need. It's an incredibly sweet thing of him to say.

The three of us look up as Logan walks into the green room. Spencer stands up and walks toward him. I almost expect some kind of altercation, but Logan stops and just looks at me. His eyes plead with me... they aren't filled with anger, but sadness.

"Spencer, it's OK," I say.

Spencer turns around and looks at me as he tries to figure out what I'm thinking. I'm not sure what I'm doing, but I feel like Logan needs to talk to me and I'm not about to deny him that.

"Are you sure?"

I nod. Spencer shrugs and steps aside.

"Can you give us a couple of minutes?" I say.

Spencer shakes his head, but walks out of the room. I'm glad that he's trying to be a friend and watch out for me, but in this moment I need to stand up for myself and tell Logan how wrong he was about the whole situation.

Dex stands up and walks out of the room. He glances over his shoulder as he walks by Logan, and I expect to feel judged by the look on his face... but there is only understanding and hope. He wants me to be happy, that much is clear and he knows I can decide what that means for me.

Logan sits down in a chair a few feet away from me, opens his mouth to say something and hesitates. I can tell this isn't going to be easy.

"What are you doing here?" I say.

"I... football is about to start... what are you doing here?"

"I just finished filming... Dex thought we should do some promo before I headed to Salem."

Logan wrinkles his brow.

"You're... you're coming back to Salem?"

"Yeah... school is about to start. I worked hard and we filmed quickly to make that happen."

Logan stands up and starts to pace. It's making me a little uneasy, but if it's going to make it easier for him to think and listen to what I'm about to say I don't really care.

"Listen, to me," I say. "I don't care what you thought may have happened, between me and Spencer... that doesn't matter now, but I want you to know my thoughts were only of you. Spencer knew I was missing the life I was pulled away from and he was trying to be nice... he's a friend, a good one, and that's all he's ever been or will ever be."

Logan stops, looks at me and runs his hand through his hair as he tries to process what I just said. I know it's a lot, neither of us expected to be having this conversation when we woke up this morning. He sits down on the couch next to me and looks into my eyes. I've missed him and this is making it even harder. I knew the chance of seeing him during school was decent... I just wasn't expecting it now.

"Amy... I... I don't even really know what to say. Sorry? I guess that's the best word... but it really doesn't convey the sadness and regret I'm feeling right now."

Logan looks at the floor and I can see him shake his head, just a little bit.

"Thing is," he says, "I'm sorry for how I acted and I hope that you can forgive me, but I don't expect it. I was mean to you and you really didn't deserve that, even if you had chosen to be with Spencer instead of me, I should have never treated you that way... especially after everything you've been through."

I almost feel like he made a fool out of me. I let myself get so worked up by what he did and I was starting to blame myself for hanging out with Spencer.

"You should have let me explain," I say. "What you did hurt me. It wasn't right, or fair for that matter, and it's something I probably won't ever forget."

Logan nods and looks at me. I can see in his eyes that he's sorry, but that doesn't change what he did.

"I know and I'm really sorry, more than I can ever explain. Please... please let me make it up to you when you come back to Salem. I still care about you and want to be with you... you just have to give me the chance to show you."

I sigh and shake my head.

"No."

"Amy, please?"

"No... there's some things in life that an apology can't fix. The past few months of my life have been hectic, crazy really, and when I was in a vulnerable point in my life you... you got so angry at me for something that didn't happen. Given how we met and how that all went down...

I thought you, of all people, would understand that I was just friends with Spencer. I guess I misjudged you."

I stand up and Logan puts his hand on my arm. I pull my arm away and walk out of the room. There's no point in him sitting around while he tries to guilt me into giving him another chance. A few months ago I would have probably fallen for that, but now... now I know better. I'm going to be a better me. I don't ever have to put up with a guy treating me like that ever again.

I round the corner and Dex and Spencer are standing in the hallway.

"Are you alright?" Spencer says.

I look at him and smile... a real smile, one that comes from the happiness of being strong.

"Never been better. Now, let's go celebrate me making a scene on national television."

CHAPTER TWENTY

The taxi driver jumps out of the car and pops the trunk as I grab my purse and get out. He sets my bags on the curb and I hand him fifty dollars. The ride from the airport was forty and I don't have any small bills left from what Dex gave me.

"Thanks, Miss."

I smile at him and lift my bags. I walk up to the front door and set them down so I can ring the bell. I stand and wait as I hear the chime ring through the house. As the door opens Jess lunges forward and throws her arms around me.

"Amy!"

"Hey."

She squeezes me tightly and I put my arms around her. It's hard to describe how good it is to see her and I know she missed me, too.

"Come in."

She grabs one of my bags and I get the other.

"How was your flight?"

"Fine," I say. "Dex paid for me to fly first class… so it wasn't as nice as the private jet, but still nice."

"Lucky."

We set my bags down on my bed and head back toward the living room. Jess sits on one end of the couch and I sit on the other. We both turn toward each other and smile.

"So," she says, "I saw the segment on Late with Lucas... that was freaking crazy. I can't believe Logan was there."

I nod. It was crazy.

"What happened after that?"

"Not much really. We celebrated that night and then Dex took me shopping, for school clothes the next day, and then I caught my flight back here. Not that exciting really."

"Clothes shopping? Did you get anything fun?"

"Some jeans, a few tops and a pair of flats... nothing crazy. It was for my birthday."

She smiles and shifts on the couch as she tries to get comfy.

"That's still nice of him."

I nod. It was nice of him, he really didn't have to buy me anything. It's crazy, I've only known Dex for such a short time, but he's become almost like a parent to me. He's not replacing my dad or my mom... he's just like another parent, one who actually cares about my well being. I'm actually going to miss him... which is not what I would have ever expected after the first few days I spent at his house when I was so mad at him. It's amazing how life changes.

"Yeah."

"So," Jess says, "how does it feel to be famous?"

"I... I'm not famous."

She raises her eyebrow and looks at me. I can tell she's trying to decide if I'm being funny or if that's what I really think. I was being honest, but I get why she might think that.

"Well, you might be in for a little bit of a surprise when classes start."

"What… what do you mean?"

"I got a couple of texts, one from a co-worker and one from a girl that I met at work, and they both were asking me if my roommate Amy was the same girl as was on Late with Lucas. A lot of people have seen that, either live or on YouTube."

I wrinkle my brow. I didn't think people really watched that show.

"Why do you look so surprised?" she says.

"Was it really that big of a deal?"

Jess laughs and reaches for a bottle of water on the coffee table.

"Think about it, Amy. You were on TV with Spencer and Logan showed up. He's a star quarterback… everyone knows who he is and people talk."

"But YouTube?"

Jess holds her hand up as she takes a drink of water and stands up.

"Let me grab my laptop."

She heads into her room and I feel panic starting to set in. What are people going to think? Will they hear about what happened between me and Logan? Ugh.

Jess sits down on the couch next to me and flips open her laptop. She opens her browser and pulls up the video. My heart skips a beat when I see the number of views. Over twenty-seven million… holy crap.

She hits play on the video, which starts with the second half of the interview.

"Jess, I really don't need to see that."

"Right," she says, closing the laptop. "Sorry."

"It's fine… I… I just can't believe how many views it has already."

I stand up and start to pace. I'm not sure what this is going to mean. I never fathomed what it would be like to be like Spencer, where everywhere he goes people recognize him, and now I have a sick feeling deep in my stomach. Is that what it's going to be like for me? I take a deep breath and sit back down.

"So... like I said, how does it feel to be famous?"

"Awful."

I feel like I'm going to throw up. It's awful to have my personal life become a public spectacle, but I guess I should've expected this. I had some vision in my mind that I was going to shoot the movie and head back to Salem and no one would know I had even done it. I know it's silly, but I thought I was going to live out the rest of my life as a regular person. Now... because of Late with Lucas, that's never going to happen.

"Don't look so worried... it's going to be fine."

Jess puts her arm around my shoulder. I just want to cry.

"I don't know what to do, Jess. I'm going to be the laughing stock of school... or the world."

"Whatever. People will have forgotten about it in no time. Don't let it get to you... and I promise it will go away."

I nod. I know she's right. There's really nothing I can do about it now other than to ride the wave that's swelling before me. I need to be more like Spencer—he would remind me that this is all a great opportunity to promote the movie and that it'll just mean that I'll make more money for myself.

"You're right."

"I know, that's why you like hanging out with me."

I roll my eyes in jest and she smiles.

"Do you have any plans for tonight?"

"Work," Jess says, her smile turning to a frown. "I tried to get it off when you texted me and said you'd be here today, but no one could cover. It's been busy this week, since school is starting and everyone that went home for the summer is back."

"It's fine... I totally get it."

"Are you sure?"

"Yes... I'm pretty tired from this week anyway. I could

stand to catch up on some sleep and rest up for the start of school."

She hops off the couch and heads toward her bedroom.

"Don't forget, next weekend is the first weekend of the year... biggest parties and I'm expecting you to be ready."

My head spins at the thought... I don't think I'm ready, but I'm not going to let her down.

"Yeah... we'll see."

Jess shakes her head and smiles.

"You've got plenty of time to get in a party mood."

"You know me."

She laughs and heads into her bedroom. I take my phone out of my pocket and check the time. It's late, almost eight. She probably has to get ready for work. I stand up from the couch and head into my bedroom as Jess heads for the bathroom.

"I've gotta get ready, but if you're awake when I get home from work we can catch up some more."

"Sure."

I know I won't be. I'm already thinking about how nice it'll be to sleep. My phone vibrates as I sit down on the bed and I look down to read it. I smile when I see it's from Dex.

Hey, hope your flight was good. You should be there by now. I just wanted to thank you again for doing such an amazing job on the film... I'll forever be in your debt. Speaking of debt, if you text me your address I can send out your check tomorrow. I want to make sure you have the money I owe you so that you can buy books and pay for school and whatever else you need.

Dex already told me that he's thinking to release the film in theaters next month. He made it sound as if things went well, the film might be paid off by the theatrical release and that Spencer and I would get royalties once it went to streaming video and DVD sometime early next year. I'm not really that worried about it, the sixty thousand he promised me for the film is more than enough to take care of my bills for a long while if I'm cautious about what I buy.

I did... just got here. Thank you, so much... you were amazing. I'll be forever grateful for everything you've done for me, Dex.

I send the text and then send a second one with the address. He gave me two hundred dollars before my flight today for the taxi and whatever else I needed to buy before he sent my check. It was unnecessary, and I told him that, but he insisted and I definitely was glad for it when it came time to pay for my taxi ride.

I flip through my phone for a couple of minutes while I wait to see if Dex is going to text back, but he doesn't. I'm sure he's already back to his hectic L.A. life.

Jess pokes her head into my room as I'm setting my phone down on my nightstand.

"I'm off to work... you good?"

"I'm good."

"I'm glad you're back," she says, smiling at me.

"Me too."

She smiles and turns to leave. I'm glad she saved my room for me... I can't imagine if she had rented it to anyone else and I had to find a new place to live. It was sweet of her to do it in the beginning and I plan on paying her for when I wasn't here, once I get my money from Dex.

I hear the front door close and I close my eyes. I would like to stay awake and unpack... and maybe even try to stay awake until Jess gets home, but I know it's a lost cause. I give in and let sleep fill my body.

CHAPTER TWENTY-ONE

I check my phone. Still no text from Spencer. It's been two days since I last saw him and I haven't heard anything from him yet. When I woke up the morning after getting here I sent him a text and he didn't even respond to that. I'm sure he's fine… Dex would have called if anything happened.

I get up and walk into the kitchen, where Jess is standing in her running outfit.

"Do you want to come?" she says.

I shake my head. There's no way in heck I'm going for a run. I'm still feeling beat up and tired from the last few months of nonstop work. It's funny because I would have never imagined being a movie to be hard work, but it was the most physically and mentally demanding thing I've ever done in my life… and I wouldn't trade that experience for anything.

"Maybe tomorrow."

She raises her eyebrow at me.

"Class starts tomorrow."

"I know… I'm trying to savor my last day of freedom and that doesn't include running with you."

"Tomorrow then… promise?"

"Promise."

She takes a sip from her water bottle and heads out the front door. I sit down on the couch and check my phone again. It's weird, I'm compulsively checking it to see if I've heard from Spencer and I can't seem to help myself. It's kind of weird, but I'm missing going to work and seeing him every day. I push the thoughts of him out of my mind and focus back on school.

Jess helped me register for classes yesterday. I didn't get everything I wanted since I waited so long, but I got four classes that I'm going to need. I'm still not sure what I'm going to major in—I thought once upon a time I wanted to be a teacher, but now I'm not so sure. It's not really a big deal, I need to take all my prerequisite classes first anyway.

It's funny, I was so devastated when I thought I wouldn't be attending State and now I'm not that excited. I guess it's going to be good… I have to go to college if I want a job where I can make money.

The doorbell rings and I get up. I wonder who could be ringing the bell? My heart starts beating faster as I realize there's a distinct chance that it's Logan. Would he really show up here? I walk to the door, as quietly as possible, and look through the peephole. It's a package delivery man and I feel like I can breathe again.

As I open the door, he lifts the huge box up and hands it to me. I glance at the name on the package and see that it's for me. I was expecting a check from Dex, but this box is giant—about four feet wide and three feet tall, maybe six inches deep. What the heck did he send me?

"Did you need me to sign?"

"Nope, you're all set."

"Thanks."

He smiles, turns and walks back toward his truck. I rest the package on my hip and close the door. It's heavy enough that I have to set it down and push it to the couch. I sit down and rip open the tape. When I pull back the cardboard flaps there's Styrofoam surrounding what's inside. I put the whole thing on the floor and pull from the open end. It slides out and smile when I see what it is. It's the painting I liked at the gallery, the one that Rodger painted, and it's in a beautiful wooden frame. There's an envelope taped to the glass in the middle of it with my name on it.

I grab the envelope and sit down on the couch. I slide my finger under the flap and rip it open. Inside there's a piece of paper folded in thirds. I open it and a check falls out and onto the couch next to me. I pick it up and smile as I look it over. Just as Dex promised, it's a check for sixty thousand dollars. I set the check on the coffee table and turn my attention to the note.

Amy,

Thank you for everything. You really helped with the film, more than I think you know. We couldn't have done it without you. Life is funny, it never really turns out the way you picture it will. I thought we had a great cast and with a turn of events we got you instead. I was scared at first… I wasn't sure you could do it, but you showed that it's important to truly believe in people. I'm sorry about everything that happened with your mom, but I'm glad that it happened. In a way, if I would have never ended up in Greenville, I would have never met her or you. The film I shot there is nothing really, but because I met you… well, I think this is it. I think this is the best film I've ever made. This film is that film that people will remember me for and you are a big part of that. I'm not sure you truly understand the impact of it, maybe I'm wrong… maybe I think it's better than it is, but time will tell.

The painting is from Rodger, he said this painting had to be yours. He said what you said about it made him feel like all the years of people telling his painting was crap made it all worth it. He didn't explain, but said you knew what he was talking about.

Take care and the best of luck with whatever path your life heads down. I hope that we meet again.

Best Wishes,

Dex

I wipe a single tear from my cheek. What he says is true. This isn't how I would have planned my life out, but I'm truly grateful for the way things worked out. I put the note next to the check and finish unpacking the painting. It really is special and I'm so grateful that Rodger wanted me to have it. I need to remember to have Dex thank him for me.

I sit back down on the couch once I've cleaned up the Styrofoam and put the box outside in the recycling. Jess walks through the front door as I unlock my phone and get ready to text Dex.

"Hey."

"How was your run?"

"Amazing, you missed a good one."

I really doubt that. I smile at her and she heads into the kitchen for water. Jess walks back into the living room, sets down her water and starts to stretch.

"Wow... nice painting. Where did that come from?"

"It's a gift from the assistant director. We had a wrap party at a gallery and I was admiring it, so he sent it to me as a gift."

She raises her eyebrows and winks at me. I can't help but laugh.

"No," I say, "he was just a really nice guy and he helped me a bunch. Dex is... well, he's Dex and I think it's been some time since he worked with a first time actor in a lead role. Rodger, the assistant director, always dumbed stuff down so that even I could understand it."

Jess finishes stretching and plops down on the couch next to me.

"I saw the clip from your movie, on Late with Lucas, and it didn't look like you needed much direction."

A wicked smile crosses her face. I knew it was only a matter of time before she brought up my kiss with Spencer. I don't mind really, it was just a kiss that had to be part of the film and nothing more. There's no point trying to convince her of that, though. She's so ridiculous.

I really missed her.

"Are you ready for tomorrow?" I say, doing my best to change the subject.

"No... I still haven't bought my books. What about you?"

"I need my books, too."

"Should we go to the bookstore now?"

"If you want. I don't have enough money yet for books... I have to go to the bank and put my check in."

Jess stands up and starts walking toward the bathroom.

"I just got paid. I'll cover you until you can get to the bank."

"Are you sure?"

"Of course. Let me just shower and we can go."

I grab my phone so that I can text Dex and thank him.

Hey, just got the package. Thank you so much, for everything. The note was sweet. You were so kind to take me in and cast me in your film, something I'll never forget. Please thank Rodger for me, it was very generous of him to give me that painting. Thanks again, for everything.

I set my phone down and pick up the check from the coffee table. Sixty thousand dollars. I know it's just a check, but I never imagined I would hold this much money in my hands. I'm really looking forward to not having to work at some crap job for a while. Best summer job ever, that's for sure. My text vibrates and I look down and read the text from Dex.

The pleasure was all mine. It's amazing what we able to accomplish in such a short amount of time. I owe it all to you and Spencer. I really hope that it makes a lot of money, not for my own sake... but because you deserve to be compensated for what your performance deserves. I know you are all about going to college, and I applaud that, but if you ever want some work or you want to do something next summer... just ask. Also, my door is always open if you want to come back to stay or visit or whatever.

The thought hadn't even crossed my mind. Ever since I went to L.A. I was convinced I wanted to get out of there

ASAP and get back to Salem for school. I don't have to decide now, though. Next summer is still a long way off and lots could change between then and now.

Thanks. I'll keep that in mind.

"You ready?"

I look up and see Jess drying off her hair. She's already dressed and looks ready to go.

"Sure," I say. "Let me just get my purse."

We head outside and get in her car. It takes longer to find a parking spot than it does to drive there, but eventually a spot opens up near the front. There are more people in the parking lot than I think there were in my entire high school and this is just for the bookstore. It's a little overwhelming.

Jess and I head into the bookstore and find her books first. Every few minutes I glance at the line, which seems to be growing the longer we are here. I'm so not ready for any of this.

"How much is the new copy?" she says.

I bend down and look at the tag.

"Two hundred fifteen."

Wow. It's amazing that a book could cost over two hundred dollars. I'm starting to feel bad that Jess said she'd cover the cost of my books.

"I guess I'm going for the used one."

She shakes her head as she grabs the slightly worn book off the shelf. It's in decent condition, but definitely used, and even that one is a hundred and fifty. Highway robbery as far as I'm concerned.

Jess nudges me and tilts her head to the left. I see two guys standing at the end of the aisle, looking at us. One of them has his phone in his hand and is pointing it at us. I wrinkle my brow and stare at them. They pause a moment longer and finally turn away.

"What was that about?" I say. "Do you know them or something?"

"No… I told you, you're famous now."

Ugh. I refuse to believe that this is what my life has become. I was on TV for a brief moment in time. I really hope Jess is right and people will forget about it. I want my five minutes of fame to be over.

"Let's get out of here."

"What about your books?"

"I'll get them in a couple of days... It's not that big of a deal."

"Are you sure?"

"Yeah," I say. "Let's just get in line so you can pay for yours."

"I have an idea."

I don't like the sound of that, but before I can say anything Jess is already making a beeline for the front of the line. I don't know what she's about to do and I have a feeling it's not going to end well.

Jess walks up to a group of three guys, who look to be about our age, who are at the front of the line.

"Hey, boys, how are you?"

They look at her and then at me before answering.

"Good," one says.

The other two just nod.

"Do you know who this is?" she says, pointing at me.

I should have guessed she was going to do this.

"Hey... aren't you that Amy girl?" one says. "The one who dated Logan Reynolds and was on TV?"

"That's her," Jess says, cutting me off as I open my mouth. "We are in kind of a hurry... do you mind if we cut?"

All three shake their heads in unison. I can't say I condone cutting or using my temporary fame to get what we want, but I'm willing to compromise if that means we can get out of here sooner rather than later. We step into line in front of them and I hear grumbles from the rest of the line. I don't turn around... I'm not about to make a bigger scene that Jess already has.

I guess I can't complain. We make it out of the

bookstore in five minutes when the line would have taken probably an hour. Jess starts laughing once we are outside and heading back to the car.

"You think you're so clever," I say.

"No... I *know* I'm clever. There's a difference."

I just shake my head. I have no idea how she doesn't get into more trouble than she already does.

It's strange... Spencer always seemed so calm when people were taking pictures of him or talking to him and I didn't mind. I can't explain it, but now that people are focused on me and he's not around it feels so different. It's almost like everything is fine when I'm with him. Spencer has this sort of calming energy. I have a feeling that the whole thing that happened on Late with Lucas would've been even worse if he wasn't sitting next to me when Logan walked out on stage.

I miss Spencer... things just don't seem the same when I'm not around him.

CHAPTER TWENTY-TWO

I sigh as I look down at my phone. My third day of classes starts in twenty minutes and I have no desire to go. Jess left already, she offered to give me a ride, but I told her I wasn't ready. She seemed a little concerned, but I told her I was fine.

The truth is, I haven't felt the same since I've been back here. I missed Jess and I was excited about school, but that was before I actually got back here. Now… now I miss L.A. more than I've ever missed anything. I'm not sure if it's that simple though. I certainly didn't fall in love with the city—I guess if I was being completely honest I miss Spencer and Dex.

School so far hasn't been what I expected it to be. It just seems like more high school, really. I guess maybe classes specific to a major are more interesting, but I really would rather be on set filming right now. I'm really not sure what to do.

I feel like a piece of me is missing.

I close my eyes and try to think about it… to think about what I really want in life—not what I'm supposed to want.

Maybe I could learn to like L.A.? The more time I

spent there the easier it got, but I also wasn't working at some crap job. I could always go to school there... there's really no reason for me to go to State other than to live with Jess, but I could always visit her.

I open my eyes and jump off my bed. I can't stay here. I pull my bag out of the closet and start tossing in all the clothes I just put away two days ago. I know it's crazy to leave, but it feels right... it feels like something I need to do. The worst that could happen is that I don't like it in L.A. and if that's the case I have my money from the movie and I could always travel a little and try and find somewhere new to live. I feel like so much of my past is a part of State and I want a fresh start.

A smile crosses my face as I zip up my bag and grab my phone to call a cab. I put my phone up to my ear as it starts to ring.

"Salem Cab, how can I help you?"

"Yeah... I need a cab to pick me up and take me to the airport."

"When?"

"As soon as possible."

I give the woman on the other end of the line my address and hang up. I wander around the house for the next few minutes making sure I've got everything I need. The only thing I'm not sure about is the painting... I can't exactly take that with me. Maybe I'll just have Jess hang onto it, for now, and have her send it to me once I get settled.

I take a piece of paper off the pad on the counter and write a note for Jess. I would text her, but she's in class by now and by the time she gets out I'll be on my flight.

Jess,

You're a great friend and an awesome roomy, but I can't stay here anymore. I just feel like my whole life since high school was all about coming here and now I'm not that same person anymore. I need more than going down the path my parents wanted for me. I want to be my own person, not the person my mom wanted me to be. I'll text you in a couple of days.

Love,

Amy.

P.S. I left the painting, if you could please ship it once I'm settled. I'll include some money for shipping when I send you what I owe for rent.

I feel like I should feel sad about leaving, Jess is really my only friend other than Spencer, but this is something I have to do.

A car honks out on the street and I peek out the front window and see a cab parked in front of the house. I grab my bag, toss my phone in my purse and lock the door behind me. The driver gets out and helps me with my bag and I get in the back seat.

"Where to?"

"The airport, please."

He nods, glances over his left shoulder and pulls away from the house. I take one look out the back window at Jess's cute little house. I tell myself I might be back here someday, but deep down I know I never will be. I'm sure the next time I see Jess it will be wherever I live.

I open my purse and take out my wallet to count my money. When I went to the bank on Monday they called Dex's bank to verify the check, because of the large amount, and they were able to give me access to the money right away. The cash I took out, plus what was left from what Dex gave me, is just over seven hundred. I was planning to buy my books with it, but I guess now it'll be my plane fare and for the taxi here and when I get there.

On the way to the airport I look up flights on my phone. There's a flight leaving for L.A., a direct flight no less, in just under an hour.

As soon as the taxi stops I jump out and hand cash to the driver as he gets my bag. I take a deep breath and run for the ticket counter. Hopefully I get there before they close check-in for the flight. I'm sure there are later flights, but right now all I can think about is putting my feet on that California ground.

There's no line at the check-in counter, which isn't a good sign. I rush up to the only counter attendant.

"Hi," I say.

"Can I help you?"

"I need to get on the flight to Los Angeles."

"Sorry, it's forty-three minutes prior to departure."

"What does that mean?"

She points to a sign behind her and I quickly skim it. *You must check in 45 minutes prior to departure or forfeit your seat on the flight.* Crap.

"Is there another flight?"

She rolls her eyes and starts to type on her computer.

"There is... I can get you on the three o'clock to Chicago and from there a connecting flight to Denver and a red-eye from Denver to Los Angeles."

My head is spinning just thinking about how much of a pain in the ass that would be.

"Please isn't there something you can do? It's only two minutes past the time."

"Three."

"Excuse me?"

"Three minutes," she says. "It was two. Now it's three."

She turns and starts to walk away.

"Please... just... stop."

She stops and turns. I know I have to come up with a perfect story if she's going to bend the rules and let me on that flight. Acting ability... don't fail me now.

"I... made a huge mistake. There's this boy," I say. "I shouldn't have left. I think I love him, but if I don't go see him now, well, I might never get a chance to really tell him how I feel. Please, can't you just let me on the flight?"

"What's his name?"

"Spencer."

I say his name without even thinking. I start to think about what I just said to the woman and... and I realize every single word of it is the honest truth.

"And you love him?"

"Ever since I met Spencer I felt like there was some connection, a spark, between us… I just always ignored it because he's Spencer and I'm just some small town girl. I never thought anything could come of it. But then… then I kissed him and I felt something deep inside me change. I thought it was just a weird feeling that would pass, but it hasn't… it's been weeks and the feeling is still there. Now it's stronger than ever and I feel like I have to be with him."

She smiles at me and walks back to the counter.

"Let's get you on that flight."

Her fingers dance on the keyboard, barely touching down, and I pass her my ID. I put my bag on the scale and wait.

"Shit," she says.

"What?"

"There's only a first class seat left… and it's six hundred and seventeen dollars."

I take my wallet out of my purse and quickly count out the cash and set it on the counter. She raises her eyebrow at the stack of cash, but doesn't say anything.

She types even more furiously than before. She stops as the printer starts and she hands me a boarding pass.

"Go."

"Thanks you, so much… It…."

"Go!"

I smile at her and run.

CHAPTER TWENTY-THREE

I get my bag off the carousel at baggage claim and head outside to look for a taxi. I'm glad my flight worked out the way it did... it was very full and it seemed like half of coach was small children. It wasn't great to spend that kind of money, but it was totally worth it. I've still not had to experience coach... next time I fly I will because I don't want to burn through the money I have. The longer I can make it last just means it's longer until I have to get another crappy job.

There's a few cabs waiting outside so I get in the one at the front of the line.

"Where to?"

I thought about where to go once I landed. I'm going to call Dex and see if he's home. If he's not around I'll go over to Spencer's and if he's not there I'll just go back to Dex's.

"Beverly Hills."

"Any specific address?"

"Not yet... I have to make a call first."

He nods and pulls away from the curb. I pull up Dex's number, hit call and hold the phone up to my ear.

"Amy? Is everything OK?"

185

It's hard to hear Dex... he's obviously somewhere really loud.

"Yeah... everything is fine."

"Can I call you back? I'm in a club and it's really loud."

"Sure."

He hangs up and I pull up Spencer's address in my phone and tell it to the taxi driver.

"Alpine Drive?"

"Yeah."

He whistles and looks at me in the rearview mirror.

"Nice neighborhood. Your folks live there?"

I frown at the rather personal question from a complete stranger.

"No... a friend."

He doesn't say anything else for the rest of the drive. I guess he caught on to the irritated tone in my voice.

The driver stops the taxi in front of Spencer's house, gets out and sets my bag on the curb. I take cash out of my wallet and hand it to him. He gets back in his car without saying anything, which is fine by me.

I take a deep breath as I try to think about what I'm going to tell Spencer. I definitely have feelings for him... I just don't know how to put them into words. He's Spencer Thomas... how's any girl like me supposed to tell him they want to be with him? I know it's a long shot, like a really long one, but I feel like if I don't tell him now I'm going to live the rest of my life regretting it.

I walk up to the door and ring the bell. With each passing moment I feel like my heart is beating faster and faster. I wait, but there's no answer. I ring the bell again... nothing. I take out my phone and pull up Spencer's number and hit call.

"Hey."

"Spencer... hey... it's Amy."

He laughs. I feel a little stupid for telling him who it was, obviously he knows.

"What's up?"

"I... I was wondering... where are you?"

I'm a little disappointed he's not home. It sounds like he's in a car and I was calling just in case he didn't hear the bell or something.

"I'm... not at home."

My heart sinks to my gut. I feel like there's only one reason why he wouldn't tell me where he was... because he's with a woman right now.

Before I can think of what to say my phone starts to beep... Dex is calling me.

"Can I call you back? Dex is beeping in."

"Sure."

I hang up and answer Dex's call.

"Hey."

"Hi, Amy. How are you?"

"I... I don't know...."

I burst into tears. I had this vision in my mind that I was going to fly back to L.A. to surprise Spencer and he was going to tell me that he couldn't live without me. Stupid, stupid, stupid. I'm an idiot. Of course Spencer is out with a woman right now, we just finished a long shoot and a publicity trip. He's probably making up for lost time.

"Amy... are you OK? Did something happen?"

I take a deep breath and force myself to stop crying. I don't want Dex to worry.

"I... I just flew into L.A. and... I don't know what I'm doing."

"What? Why? What happened?"

"Nothing... happened... not really. I just... I don't know. Where are you?"

"I'm in New York... a friend was having a party so I decided to go. I'm so sorry that I can't be there. I'll head to the airport right now and get on the next flight."

I smile. He's such a good guy.

"No... I'm fine. That's not necessary."

"Are you sure?"

"Yeah, I'll be OK."

"Only if you're sure. I can call Gina and have her let you in the house. Where are you right now?"

I hesitate. I don't really want to tell him… I'm embarrassed now that Spencer isn't here.

"I… have you talked to Spencer?"

"No. Why?"

I take a deep breath and try not to think about my phone call with Spencer.

"I called you from a taxi and since you weren't home I had them take me to Spencer's, but he's not here. I called him, but he wouldn't tell me where he was."

"OK… don't move. I'm going to call him and if I can't reach him I'll call Gina and have her pick you up there and take you to my house."

"Thank you, Dex."

"Of course. Sit tight."

I hang up and sit down on the front step of Spencer's house. It's a nice night, maybe a little warm for my taste, still not as hot as earlier in the summer.

My phone rings and I look down, expecting to see it's from Dex, but Spencer's name and number pop up.

"Hello?"

"Amy, are you at my house?"

I guess Dex must have called him and told him.

"Yes."

"What are you doing there?"

"I… I came back to L.A. and Dex wasn't home so I came here to see if you were around."

He starts laughing.

"What's so funny?" I say.

"You should go to Dex's… it's going to take me a few hours to get back."

I don't even want to ask where he is that he needs a few hours to get back.

"It's fine, don't hurry back. Keep… keep doing whatever it was you were doing."

"Amy… the reason I didn't want to tell you where I

was… well, I'm in Salem."

"What?"

My mind races as I try to think of a reason for him to be there.

"Why are you there?" I say.

"I… I wanted to talk to you and I thought it would be best to do in person."

A car pulls up in front of Spencer's house and I look up. It's Gina's car. She rolls down the window and waves.

"Gina is here."

"Go to Dex's… I'm heading back to the airport right now. I'll be there as soon as I can."

"But what… what was so important that you flew to Salem?"

"Please, Amy, just go to Dex's and I'll explain when I get there."

"OK."

"I'll see you soon," he says.

I wonder what he could possibly want to talk to me about. I wonder if he has some kind of feelings for me. If that was the case, why didn't he say anything before? I try not to think about it… there's no reason, he's not going to be here for hours and I can't get myself all worked up if it turns out to be nothing. There's a possibility that he had some film project he wanted to talk to me about in person or something.

I stand up, grab my bag and head toward Gina's car. This is going to be the longest few hours of my life.

CHAPTER TWENTY-FOUR

I look down at my phone and reread the text from Spencer.

Just landed. On my way.

Short and to the point. The last few hours waiting for Spencer have seemed like the longest of my life—I just want him to get here before I lose the courage to tell him how I feel. The entire time since I talked to him all I can think about is what he wants to say to me. I can't decide which one of us should go first. If I go first and tell him how I feel he might have something completely different on his mind. If he goes first and tells me something like he met some woman… well, that would just break my heart. I think I need to just go first and so that I'm certain I won't hold back and not tell him how I really feel.

I force myself to not think about all of the ways talking to Spencer could go horribly wrong. I take a deep breath and try to calm myself down. I know he's going to be here at any moment and I want to be in a good space emotionally.

The doorbell rings and I stand up. I feel dizzy and have to close my eyes. I put my hand on my chest and feel the pounding of my heart. The doorbell rings a second time and I head downstairs to get it. Gina asked if she should stay, but I sent her home... I don't want anyone to witness what's about to happen in case I make a complete fool of myself.

He rings the doorbell a third time as I put my hand on the handle and pull it open. Spencer steps inside and wraps his arms around me before I say anything. He sighs as he hugs me.

"Hi." he says.

"Hi."

Spencer lets me go and I close the door. I follow him into the living room and sit down on the couch, leaving about a foot between us.

"I need to tell you something," I say.

"Alright, but I need to tell you something first."

Crap. I open my mouth to try and start talking first, but he starts before I can even think of what to say.

"The thing is, Amy... I didn't tell my mom we're just friends because... well, it's painful, but I know that I need to tell you."

"Spencer, you don't have t...."

"Amy, please... before I lose my nerve. My dad and my sister... they died, about seven years ago and I don't really talk about it. It was when I was still living in Colorado and thinking about moving to L.A. to be an actor. I was almost sixteen at the time... I won't ever forget that day. My dad, he picked my sister up from soccer practice and they were heading home and...."

A tear rolls down his cheek and I scoot close to him on the couch and put my hand on his arm.

"And... a drunk driver came across the center line and hit them head-on at sixty. My dad and my sister died, Amy, and it was awful. I've... I've never seen my mom as happy since before then as when she assumed we were together."

I feel terrible for thinking that he had some less legitimate reason for holding back. I get it now... I just wish he would have told me, but I get why he didn't.

Spencer takes a deep breath and turns to me. I reach up and wipe a tear from his face. I force myself to smile for no other reason than to try and cheer him up.

"The thing is... it made me realize how short life is. It was hard for me to move to L.A., but I knew I had to go after my dream of becoming an actor... my dad wouldn't have wanted me to do anything else. He believed in me more than anyone."

I can feel tears starting to well in my eyes. I take a deep breath and calm myself down as I try not cry.

"Why did you go to Salem? You could have told me that over the phone," I say.

Spencer shakes his head and looks deep into my eyes.

"It's because of that... that awful tragedy. Like I said, it made me realize how short life is... and the moment you got on that plane and left... well, I felt like a part of me had been ripped out and I would never be the same. Even if me telling you this leads nowhere... well, I had to try... I had to tell you how I feel. Amy, spending every day with you these last couple months has been the most amazing time in my life and I don't want to be without you. I need to be with you."

I didn't expect him to feel that way about me.

I move even closer to Spencer and put my arms around his neck. I press my lips against his and my world spins as a spark deep inside me bursts into a hot heat. I was so worried that a guy like Spencer couldn't like a girl like me, when really he felt the same way about me. He breaks the kiss, runs his hand through my hair and brushes it behind my ear.

"Now... why the heck did you show up at my house?"

That undeniable confidence is back in his voice. I can feel my cheeks burning as he looks at me.

"I... I realized that I wasn't supposed to be in Salem. I knew that I needed to tell you how I felt and that if I didn't I would probably regret it the rest of my life."

He laughs and kisses me again. This time I feel his

tongue as he slips it into my mouth and I press mine against it. I break the kiss and sit back.

"How come you waited so long to say something?" I say.

"Me? Why is it always the guy's job?"

"I don't know… but you're Spencer Thomas. It's a little intimidating trying to tell you that I want to be with you. Do you have any idea what that's like?"

He moves in for another kiss, but slides his mouth to my ear instead. Spencer wraps his arms around me as his warm breath falls on my neck.

"I'm just Spencer and you're just Amy. That's all that matters."

I smile as he kisses my neck. I don't know what my future holds, but I have a pretty good feeling that Mr. Thomas is going to have a pretty prominent role in it and I couldn't be happier.

~~~

Thank you for reading Endless Love. I hope that you enjoyed The Love Series. If you want to be notified when my next book comes out you can join my email list by visiting http://eepurl.com/xbe7z

Also, if you want to find out more about me or one of my other books, please visit my website www.emmakeene.com

ABOUT THE AUTHOR

I live in beautiful Seattle, WA with my amazing, supportive husband and our two German Shepherds that truly believe it's all about them. I love the rain and it gives me plenty of time to read and write.

54941708R00121

Made in the USA
Charleston, SC
13 April 2016